Meema,

Letters HOME

You already Know!!! . . .

♡ M

Letters HOME

Maggie Stephens-Dykes

Library of Congress Control Number:		2012921881
ISBN:	Hardcover	978-1-4797-4860-0
	Softcover	978-1-4797-4859-4
	Ebook	978-1-4797-4861-7

This book was printed in the United States of America.

To order additional copies of this book, contact:
Xlibris Corporation
1-888-795-4274
www.Xlibris.com
Orders@Xlibris.com
123881

". . . Am I my brother's keeper?"

Genesis 4:9

This is for them!

Save Me, Father, From Myself! I Am On A Path Of Destruction To Which I Know No Bounds.

By the time I cried those words, I had hit rock bottom—spiritually, emotionally, and morally. Half naked on the bathroom floor of my favorite beachfront resort, I could not stop the room from spinning. Blood speckled the puddle of vomit that lay on the beautiful white marble beneath me. The symbiosis of how far I fell eternally lives grouted in time. My cries for help bounced off soundproof walls. I lay there, wondering how I got to such a low point in my life! After all, wasn't I living the American dream? A loving husband (his pain in the butt self), two beautiful children (their pain in the butt selves), two dogs (just like having two additional children), cars, and the crown jewel—the white picket fence surrounding a beautiful two-story gray-and-white wide-line high ranch (housework, housework, and more housework.) Everything's perfect, right? Wrong!

When I was in my prescription-drug-induced haze, those things were true. Time slowed to complete everything I needed to do. At least that was the false perception I had. Go to class, work, get home, put on my June Cleaver dress and apron. How was it that she never had a stain on that perfectly starched frock? And don't forget about that perfectly coiffed hair of hers, there was never a strand out of place either. At those times, I imagined I was the black version of her. However, when I looked in the mirror, all I saw was me in a pair of raggedy sweatpants and a coffee-stained T-shirt, with my hair pulled back in a ponytail. I often wondered what she had on after the director yelled cut! By the time he yelled cut, what did her house actually look like? For all we know, she could have belonged on *Hoarders*. In the television show, all her laundry was miraculously washed, dried, folded, and neatly put away, instead of dressing from the pile of clothes that lay on the couch. (How many times do I have to ask the kids to put their clothes away before I end up doing it? I'll just do it tomorrow, less headache.) On the show, dinner was cooked and served by six o'clock, instead of eating at the drive-through window three to four times a week! (It was quicker to eat in the car.) If only I had heeded my mother-in-law's advice, I would not be lying on this cold-ass floor dying, reliving these memories I thought I packed away and buried deep in a closet with the rest of my skeletons!

She said (By the way, her name is Maggie also! I know *weird*—what's even weirder is my husband and his father both share the same name. Two pairs, I thought that was supposed to beat a full house or something? My son being a third, I warned him not to even think of bringing anyone home with the initial "M"), "You have got to stop trying to be supermom and a super wife. It is going to drive you crazy. Why does everything have to be perfect with you? There is no such thing, my dear. You cannot be all things for everybody else and have nothing left for you!"

But faith was a gift that I had yet to receive. Especially in myself, what I did was never enough. Being a wife, being a mother (ladies, you know everything that entails), being a graduate student, winning academic awards, and working as the assistant to the director of education at the graduate school I attended, everything for everyone else could not fill my gaping hole of inadequacy. The higher I piled my plate of life, the more I felt alive. But after each course I devoured, I felt unfilled. That bottomless pit of discontent led to a nasty prescription drug addiction.

I returned from the beach alone to sneak another mix of magic pills, followed by a lovely glass of wine from the bottle I had hidden in my suitcase. The doctor telling me to have a glass every night before bed to help me relax was all the permission I needed. Enough time had not elapsed between abuses. Subsequently, the lethal mix of euphoria betrayed me. My intermingling of lies and deceit had come to an end. I embraced death like a lover in the night as the memories of loved ones swirled around me. My eyes closed as the tears rolled down my face at the thought of the life I wasted. I drew my last breath as my requiem flashed before me. It was not the celebration I romanced, but disheartening as those I loved dearly grieved.

Being that I never anticipated the backlash that followed the release of *On the Morrow.* Not from them anyway. My brothers and sisters completely stopped talking to me. It was said I betrayed them. "You shouldn't be telling such private things." Or "Some things should not be repeated." As well as "You have people laughing at us, Maggie. What were you thinking?" Mother followed suit after her boyfriend read it and discovered he was not in it. It was not about him, any of them! But they could not understand that.

It was about me and my healing process. Writing the book was not about airing dirty laundry. It was the complete opposite. I did not want to spend what time I had left on this rock being angry. Actually it was about forgiveness and moving forward. But by the time it was published, we all had gone in different directions. Some wandered down one-way streets unable to let go of the past; others traveled down wrong ways, speeding through caution lights, spinning their wheels in place committing old crimes and losing time. A few of us, unable to decide which direction to travel, sat at the intersection as the traffic light continuously changed. (If you beep that horn one more time, I swear I am going to . . . *go around, dammit!*) Lost and incapable of navigating the byways and highways successfully, the remaining of us relies on a GPS. Me, I'm at the crossroads.

I wish they understood my intent so we could have moved past all the hurt and pain. Now it is too late; they will never know my true intent. So, I am going to take you through these memories of mine chronologically, as I saw them unfold before me, if I can, because these recollections are personal and intermingle. Pay close attention and follow along because although many of them are funny in a sadomasochistic way, many are not, and I do not think I will be able to tell them twice. If you think I'm a neurotic, continue reading and learn how Mother truly messed them up. This is their story! Through it, you may even walk away with a greater understanding of yourself. I wish I had!

Dearest Paige,

Sister, your sacrifices have not gone unnoticed. Even though you think they did. What you did not know was I gathered them all and saved them so one day I could thank you for each and every one.

You thought you were alone and no one heard your cries in the darkest of night. But I sat in shadow listening intently, trying to figure out a way to comfort you. Your struggles were always my plight. Your smiles are my joy. I know your tears watered my garden of life. Your love enabled me to blossom and encouraged me to grow.

Many think it weird and ask why as a grown woman, I still kiss you gently upon your lips when I see you. I smile and relish in the fact that I know something others don't, a secret that could never be understood by outsiders. As a child, I watched for those times when you were distant, so far adrift that I thought I'd never see you again.

Do you remember, I would climb upon your lap, take your troubled face in my small hands, pull your face to mine, close my eyes, and kiss your lips? When I opened my eyes, there you were again. Smiling back at me, though exhausted from your journey, of winding roads and rocky paths, in thickets of brush that scraped and scratched your beautiful brown skin. Each and every time, my kisses freed you from demons that held you captive. Futility trying to keep you from me! If you don't remember, it's because of all those drugs you did, fried your brain, bitch!

Forever my "Sullwa" with that banging-ass Afro!

I knew it would be hard writing about you, most likely the hardest of them all. The tears are already soaking my shirt.

Ghetto Fabulous

One of my favorite memories of Paige would have to be when I was in kindergarten. I was chosen to play Rosa Parks in honor of Black History. We did not get an entire month to celebrate our heritage. In 1974 it was more like a day, if that. The teachers usually read a book about Dr. Martin Luther King Jr., Rosa Parks, Ruby Brooks, or Harriet Tubman. The students colored a picture of their face and wrote a sentence or two about why it is important to remember them. My teacher, however, Mrs. G, was a true rebel, the kind of teacher who made sure you learned, willingly or otherwise. Her yard ruler met the top of my head many times for talking in class. It defied all the laws of physics, and no matter how far away she was it always made contact. One time she went to the main office, and I saw it as an opportunity to speak freely. Before I could get one word out, her arm stretched out of the office, down the hall, around the corner, and through the door. She whacked me on the head so hard; I fell back into my seat.

A minute later her body followed. "Maggie, didn't I tell you no talking? Come here."

"I'm not finished coloring."

"If you hadn't been talking, you would have been. You can finish it during recess."

"But—"

"But nothing, now."

The walk to her desk took an eternity. My imagination ran wild at the thought of what was going to happen when I reached the big brown mammoth monstrosity she sat behind. Fear rolled down my face and plopped on the floor. I hated when she summoned me. She stood toe-to-toe with me, towering over me like a lone Amazon tree in a forest of miniatures, forcing me to look up at her as she scowled down at me. Although extremely beautiful, it was overshadowed by her cold persona.

With the exception of an occasional snicker at my bastardization from one of the twins who ate paste, the class was so silent you could hear a pin drop. They were just as afraid as I was.

As I approached, I wondered how long it took her to wind that bun in such a tight ball. Her caramel skin cracked around the eyes, no doubt from sneering at each and every infraction made by the students. Something she, I'm sure, later regretted!

"I was just approved by the principal to put on a play in tribute to, instead of just remembering, Black History." Haphazardly she shuffled papers around, as she organized her messy desk. "Since you like to talk so much, I want you to audition for the lead role. The play will not be just for the school, but the community as well. So tell your Mother and family to come."

Deep down, I think she was trying to be funny. She knew Mother was not going to come. When I was commanded to tell her she was needed at school, I either told Paige or made up an excuse why she could not make it. Do you know how many times Mother came staggering in my class with her wig twisted? None! Until now I kept our dirty laundry where it belonged.

To Mrs. G's surprise, I auditioned and not only scored the starring role, but also gave an Academy Award-winning performance as Mrs. Rosa Parks herself! After it was over, the class exited the stage. Paige stood there smiling a big cheesy smile, crying, and clapping. I ran off the line and jumped into her arms. She caught me in midair and kissed me a million and one times. It was truly one of those moments you see on television. She hugged and squeezed me so tight; her tears wet the side of my face.

The only words she managed to say were "You did such a good job. I'm so proud of you."

I will never forget that moment! She was the only one from my family that showed up. It just so happened a talent scout was in the audience and approached Paige about putting me in a commercial. She gave him our address and told him he needed to speak with Mother. When the scout came to the house, Tack answered the door. He and Mother were drunk out of their mind. Needless to say, Hollywood never came calling again!

Paige is the oldest of the seven of us. She reminds us of that fact to this day. As if the last fifty-plus years telling us fell on deaf ears. She is bossy to say the least, controlling to a fault, and a neat freak. If you look up obsessive-compulsive disorder in the dictionary, you will see her picture. Not to mention that whoever came up with the diagnosis "bipolar disorder" met her and coined the phrase. It explains a lot now, because hindsight is better than foresight. But a diagnosis would not make a difference to us. We did not need a label to tell us that she is straight crazy. Growing up, crazy was not on the bus, it lived right upstairs. When I say crazy, I do not mean having a conversation with herself and boiling cats. Nothing like that. We deemed her crazy because of the way she reacts to certain situations. Usually something surrounding one of us! I will tell you what though, if you were in a bind, she will be the first one right by your side. Knee-deep in the trenches, no matter what! It is her love of us that held her back so long. A love that had to make sure we were all okay before she could begin to think of being happy. She was unhappy for a long time. But God has a funny way of turning things around when you least expect it.

Growing up, we called her baby doll. Of all my sisters, she was the one who cared about the image she projected, aesthetically that is. Lord knows, she thinks she has the right to act the fool wherever she is, or with whomever is in her company. As long as she looks good doing it! When you go out with her, you better have a Xanax ready to calm your nerves. She was always like that, short-fused and quick to react. The world is on her time. There is a twelve-year gap between us, so I learned a lot from her. She never kept anything from me. Good, bad, and everything in between!

When I was little, I loved to watch her prepare to go out. Being one of her many rituals, it literally took hours! The first thing she did was lay out her clothing. No matter what it was, it was clean, crisp, and pristine. From her bell-bottom pants, platform shoes, and polyester shirt with the wide lapel, to her apple jack hat. Next, she undressed and put on her fake red Chinese silk robe. Depending on where she was going, dictated the hair do. If she was hanging with her "crew," she put a scarf on to protect that gravity defying Afro of hers. Her crew was named SWATT, which stood for Sweet Wonderful Aware Terrible and Treacherous. Her name was Coke, a name that would follow her for years. However, if she was going on a date, she meticulously rolled it. She took the utmost time to incorporate each and every strand onto its curler. There would be a million pink sponge rollers on the top of her head. Then she applied a thick white layer of Noxzema all over her face as she ran a bath. She looked like someone hit her in the face with a whip cream pie.

Before she slid into the tub, she painstakingly scrubbed her face as if she was trying to remove a shade of black. The first time I saw the movie *Mommie Dearest,* I thought they stole the opening scene from her. Paige always tested the water with her big toe before totally submerging herself. After she stepped out of the tub, she rewashed her feet before she put them in the slippers that matched her robe. She thoroughly oiled herself and put the robe back on. Next, she painted her fingernails and toenails. Back then there was no Ms. Kim, or money to get a mani-pedi for that matter.

I will be damned if she did not paint them like they were airbrushed. After they dried, she combed her hair. Either picked it to perfection or styled it like she was attending a grand affair. I always liked when she wore her Afro parted down the middle, with a bobby pin holding down each side of her hair. Last, but not least, her makeup. She never went anywhere without it. We still tease her because she applies it the same way she did thirty years ago.

Now you know it is time for a change. It is in change we find purpose, but change is not easy for her. It has to be done gradually. If it is too fast, it throws off her equilibrium and messes up her entire day. I told you she is a ritualistic person, a creature of habit. Now as an adult, I understand that these *habits* were exegetical behaviors she created to survive what could have broken most hard-core veterans. They kept order in her order less world.

Although some of her rituals have evolved since the seventies, lining her lips with a black eye liner and putting on every piece of jewelry she owns has not. Though now her Afro is fried, dyed, and laid to the side. One month it's blonde, and the next, it's a shade of red.

I always felt safe with Paige. She took on the role of our mother at a very young age. It was a role she took very seriously. When you see a person constantly caring for you, it is natural to become attached. For many years, I actually thought she was my mother because I was always with her. In my mind, I thought she gave birth to me and said Mother was my mother.

One day I asked her, "Are you really my mother?"

She smiled and replied, "No, silly girl. I'm not your mother. I'm only twelve years older than you are! I'm your sister, but you'll always be my baby."

At the time, I did not know what that meant. Though she loved us all, I always thought she loved me more because she spoiled me with love and gifts. I can remember once I needed school clothes and supplies. Mother was on a binge and was not able to go shopping. She gave Paige and one of the other "SWATT" members' money.

As I sat playing with my doll, Paige said, "Mother, what am I supposed to get with this?"

Her voice slurred. "Whatever you can, it's all I have."

"Why didn't you call her father and ask him for money?"

"Maggie knew she was supposed to take her ass out there to get money from him, and she wouldn't go. I told her if she didn't go get that money, she was going to be outta luck. I don't have it, dammit."

"It's not her responsibility to get money from him. You need to try to find out why you have to make her go out there."

"She goes when *she* wants something."

"No, she doesn't. You make her go! You know what, just give me the money and let me get out of here. I hope you take a nap before I get back."

"You don't tell me what to do."

"Maggie, come here."

"Yes, Swulla."

"Stay in the house until Roddy comes home, then you can go out and play. I'll be back later. Don't go anywhere with Mother or anybody else."

"You don't have to tell her not to go with me. I wasn't going anywhere anyway. But if I was, she's my damn child. Where I go, she goes."

"You heard what I said, right?"

"Yes, Swulla."

To say Paige and Mother had a contentious relationship is an understatement. Mother burdened her with responsibilities she neglected. Paige especially had a problem leaving me alone with Mother when she was drunk ever since she lost me for one whole day. She had been drinking and entertaining all morning. Time and alcohol consumption caught up to her. After she awoke, I was gone. Paige panicked when Mother could not tell her who had been at the house, more or less how long I had been gone. Hours passed like minutes. Search parties made up of family and friends left no bush unturned. Looking everywhere they thought I might be and every place I should not be. Now inconsolable, she succumbed to her worst fear. Just when she thought all was lost, she just asked. God, being bigger than her biggest fear, manifested her request. For the simple reason that what is impossible for man is always possible for Him.

Someone shouted in the crowd, "I found her, Paige. I found her."

"Where is she then?"

"In a shed on Sherman Street."

"Ohhh God, noooo."

"No, she's all right. She's fine. But—"

"But what, Cheryl, what?"

"She's with Big Tittie Dot."

"Dottie?"

"She wouldn't give her to me. I tried to take her, but Dot fought me, and Maggie started screaming, so I told her I was coming to get you. Come on."

When Paige opened that shed door, I was more afraid of what she would do to Dottie than happy I was going home. "Big Tittie Dot" was one of the not-so-homeless people I fed with Mother's leftovers on the side of the "two o'clock store" on Prospect Avenue. Her breast were humongous, hence the name. She had a terrible stammer, and when she became excited, you could not understand a word she said. But I loved her. She was the sweetest person you ever wanted to meet. I am not sure to whom she was related, or where she lived. Uncle Charlie introduced Dot to us. They dated for many years on and off. So she would visit us regularly. As soon as she saw me, she would stretch out her arms, and I would run and jump right into those breast. Paige did not like for her to kiss me because her hygiene was not the best.

"Dot, let her go. Maggie, come to me!"

"IIIIIII, tri, tri, tri, to, to, to . . ."

"Paige, don't hit her. It's not her fault."

"AAAAHHH . . . ahhhhhahh . . . IIIIII, tried to . . . to . . . to . . ."

Dottie cowered in the corner of the shed huddled there broken, because the world could not understand her. But I did. You just had to be patient and listen. That is the great thing about children. They have all the time in the world. Unfortunately, once the wide-eyed innocence of a child is gone, so is the magic of what makes the world special. For with time comes wisdom. Wisdom, however, has a way of making a cynic of us all. Therefore, being different in a place in which everyone else seems to be the same made you an easy target. I walked over to Dot and took her hand.

"Mother fell asleep, so Dottie took me for a walk. Those bad kids from the other end of Maplewood Drive saw us and beat her up. We ran, and they chased us. They threw rocks at us and hit me here. It hurts, Paige."

"How did you end up in a shed on Sherman Street? This is the other side of town!"

"It's where she comes to hide when they hurt her. This is her safe place because they beat her every time they see her."

"Come on out, you too, Dottie. I'm sorry, come on."

"I waaa . . . was keep . . . keeping her safe for you."

"I know. Come to the house to clean yourself up and get something to cat."

"You mad at me, Paige?"

She picked me up and swung me around and around. "No, baby girl, I just missed you so much I had to find you. No one else knows you like to be twirl around like a Ferris wheel."

"I knew you'd come. I told Dot, right, Dot? I told you she would come. Are you going to beat those bad kids up for hurting me and Dot?"

"I sure am, baby!"

"Can I take a bath when I get home, my dress is dirty?"

"With all the bubbles you want."

"Oh, can Dot have some of Mother's *coffee*? I told her I would ask because she loves *coffee*."

"When we get home, I'll make her some."

"Good, because she said it helps settle her nerves!"

That must have been some strong-ass *coffee* because she left our house happy as all get out! But now that I think about it, I don't remember Paige or Mother brewing coffee that night? Dot was never bothered again.

When Paige and her friend returned from "shopping," they had over five hundred dollars' worth of clothing and supplies. Now sober, the red flag went up in Mother's head. I could hear her telling Paige she was going to jail. As usual, Paige ignored her. She called me into the living room. A big black garbage bag sat in the middle of the floor.

"Sit down and close your eyes. I have a surprise for you." When I complied, she sang, "Open your eyes!" Clothes and supplies fell on the floor. "Whose gonna be the prettiest girl in school?"

"Take it back, Swulla. I don't want you to go to jail." My crocodile tears extinguished her fiery temperament. She could never stand to see me cry. And I knew it. So I used it to my advantage. (I still do.)

I stared at her nails to see what color they were as she took my little face in her large hands and wiped away the bane of her existence. Then she kissed my wet cheeks and tickled me. "I'm not going to jail. Who would get you dressed in all these pretty clothes for school? Or put these barrettes in your hair? Now take this and go try it on. As soon as I saw it, I knew you would look so pretty in them, their coveralls."

In that moment, the tradition of wearing either coverall pants or a coverall dress on the first day of school was born. By the fifth grade,

I was so over it. I ran to my room. As I put the outfit on, I could hear Mother and Paige doing what they did best.

"If the police come looking for you, I'm going to tell them where you are. I am not going to lie or go to jail for anyone."

"Believe me, I know that already. But we can lie for you, right? Don't forget who kept your ass out of jail when you shot her father. You think I care if I go to jail? As long as she has what she needs for school. Lord knows you never did it, for any of us!"

Mother taunted, "Here we go—poor Paige . . ." And she threw a shoe at her. She lit a cigarette. "Give me back a hundred dollars of the money I gave you. You can keep the eighty and split it with Gloria."

"No, I already spent some of it and split the rest with Gloria."

"Spent it on what, *Paige*?"

"How do you think I got to the store and back, *Mother*?"

"On the bus!"

"With a garbage bag full of stolen shit? You need to stop drinking."

"Well, how much do you have left?"

When Paige went out with her friends, I became very upset. I hated to see her go, because sometimes she would not return for two or three days. At sixteen, no one should disappear for such stretches of time. Especially those, who have no one looking for them. It became, that every time she went out I thought she would be gone forever. At five I could not separate what Mother said out of drunken anger was not what she meant verbatim.

Unlike most siblings, she never left if I was upset. No matter how many of her friends told her to just leave me I would be all right. If I was upset, she stayed until I calmed down and fell asleep, in her bed. When she came home, I would still be there, even if it were three days later.

She'd move me over, climb in, and curl up next to me. Paige protected me from all the things that went bump in the night. It was usually Mother doing the drunk-monkey shuffle as she stumble into things making sure not a spoon was left in her sink. Instead of searching for dirty utensils, she should have been making sure all her children were in their beds. It was after all 10:00 p.m., and she didn't know where her children were!

Paige quit school, in the twelfth grade, at the eleventh hour. One month before graduation. She said she was overwhelmed from taking care of us. I am sure she will beg to differ, but it was that fear of change. She was afraid of what would come after she graduated. Growing up and possibly leaving us. She could not do that. Previous traumatizing events scared her. Not wanting such ugliness to ever touch us prevailed. Every time something changed, it fell upon her. The only way she knew how to stop change was to check out of life. If you do not play, you cannot lose. Self-sabotage became her best friend. The walls she built around her heart were fortified, causing her to become angry at the world. Time being continual in which events happen quickly passed her by. Her self-imposed isolation kept her stuck in pockets of time. Thus her world became one-dimensional. Anything good that happened to her was usually a surprise. I have learned from firsthand experience that a person can become very dark when they only expect bad things to happen. I watched as the light gradually faded from her eyes. Her dismal view manifested in deviant ways.

Unfortunately for her, she saw way too much, from an early age. She was the result of a loveless relationship rout with violence. If one is actually a product of their environment, one cannot possibly expect her to have been a person filled with ardent zeal.

In her defense, Mother tried to leave Paige's father's violent fist many times. She knew it was just a matter of time before his rage toward her would not be sated. The first time she fled she had a black eye, busted lip, bloody nose, bruises on her chest, arms, and legs. She felt that Paige being only two years old would slow her down. So she decided to leave her with Grandma Lily. If you read the last book, you know that was not such a good idea. Mother dropped her off and went to New York. The plan was to retrieve Paige once she was settled.

Three days after dropping her off, my sister was hospitalized with third-degree burns, over forty percent of her body. The skin on her back, upper arms, and thighs were burned completely off due to negligence. Grandmother was preparing food for her juke joint. A frying pan of oil was heating on the stovetop. Paige, left unattended, tugged at the dangling handle just enough to tilt the pan off its axis. The hot oil rolled down her tender skin like molten lava down a grassy knoll, incinerating everything in its violent path.

The doctors did not think she would survive. Mother returned to the welcoming fist of a man who was more upset that she tried to leave him than his child being in critical condition. The next two years were painful for Mother and Paige. Both scared, it caused them a lifetime of ignominy and insecurity.

Her burned flesh disfigured more than just her young tender skin, but both their outlooks on life, as well. Demonic voices constantly telling one she was too hideous for anyone to love, and the other, she had to stop making him angry. Being dejected by her mother, created a warped reality of not being worthy of love. Though two different voices, they carried the same message in concert. Ultimately becoming so loud they could not hear anything else.

Mother successfully fled to New York at the age of eighteen with Paige on her hip and Richard in her belly. They lived hand to mouth, and things quickly worsened. Mother was in a new relationship months after giving birth. She left the two of them behind to be cared for by her cousin and his wife. There they thrived, living the life, as children should. Attending church every Sunday and even a few days a week. Once again a transitory taste of normalcy was short-lived.

However, change changed for her again, after Mother returned to get them, ready to give birth, for the third time. She uprooted them and moved to New Jersey. However brief, Paige experienced stability, from a man, Mother says was the nicest person she ever met. Nevertheless, more changes came when that relationship failed. Mother had a nervous breakdown, thus leaving them behind again. Paige not only cared for herself and Richard, but also cared for her newborn sister, Ann.

It became increasingly difficult to place them. Paige often attacked whoever tried to attend to her siblings. She would throw herself on the floor or hit the closest person to her. As well as throw things at them, scream profanities, and threaten to kill them. It was daunting to perform the simplest tasks. Unfortunately that would become her way of dealing with everything, and not just as a child!

When Mother returned to get them, she was in another relationship. The four of them moved to Bridgehampton, New York. They lived in a big beautiful house all the while a new one was being built from the ground up on Three Mile Harbor in Easthampton. She drove luxury cars and wore designer clothing. Mother was the arm piece of a wealthy entrepreneur with whom she had grown up with. He spoiled her and the children, but it didn't come without cost especially for Paige. She and her younger siblings were left with whoever would care for them. Mother now lived a party lifestyle. She had truly become her mother's daughter, often gone and rarely home. When she was at home, the party followed her there. Unfortunately not everyone who watched the children was nice. Some had ulterior motives of fulfilling deviant appetites.

One night after partying, Lauren drove me home. At that time, she did not drink, so she was always the designated driver. Paige decided to spend the night with me. She was in a terrible mood, but I knew exactly what would make her feel better. She liked for me to cook her most favorite thing in the world, French fries. Oh no, not the ones that come precut and frozen in the bag. I had to peel, slice, and deep-fry the potatoes as she watched. Though time consuming, I did not necessarily mind, unless I was just too fucked up to carry out her demand. Then it became a battle of the wills! Unfortunately there has been an occasion or two, where, I was jarred awake to the blaring sound of the fire alarm and the house full of smoke. So to avoid smoke inhalation, I usually let her win. Fortunately for me, after we moved to North Carolina, Mother left town a lot. During these times, Paige and I would talk about everything and nothing. This one particular night we sat at the table, and she began to speak. She told me a story about a male friend of Mother's who babysat when she went out. Yes, you know where this is going! Out of love and respect for my sister, I choose to omit the gory details. But I'm sure you can use your imagination as to what happened.

It is during these periods that I am five, and she is seventeen again. I'd sit on her lap and give her a big kiss and say, "You know why you are the best sister in the world?"

She could only shake her head, her tearful eyes pleading for the answer.

"Because you . . ."

You didn't think I was going to tell you what I said, did you? Sorry, that's just for her and me to know! Though less often, these days those nasty demons still rear their ugly head. Though I can no longer climb up and sit in her lap, I still tell her why she is the best big sister in the world. Paige is kicking sixty in the ass, and she's not as strong as she likes to think she is! All right, all right, I have put on quite a few pounds, and my ass is a bit wider, thus flatter, than it used to be. It's just not fair that Ann got all the booty and left the three of us hanging like that. That bitch never did like to share; more on her later.

By the age of twelve, Paige cared for herself, plus six additional children, had watched Mother go through three failed relationships, entering the forth, and spiral out of control with alcohol. One situation after the next became more abusive than the latter, in one way, shape, or form. She saw and endured way too much for her young mind to handle. It was bound to come out somehow.

By her early teenage years, she was sexually active (of her own account), ran away several times, was drinking, smoking, and dabbling with drugs. Yes, it was the seventies—a time of the aforementioned, but by fifteen she was pregnant; and Mother did not know until she was almost due. She took her to a doctor and was told that the baby girl she carried was dead. The doctors told her she would not be able to have any more children. Mother told her if she ever saw the father of the child again, she would send her to live with Grandma Lily. Young love, lost out to a much stronger bond. The night she came from the hospital, she saw Mother shoot my father five times as he tried to escape out of the bathroom window. He left Mother's best friend in their bed to fend for herself. (Maybe that's where I get it from. I cannot keep a friend to my name. Nah, I would have shot them both!)

Needless to say, that relationship ended, and she moved the family to Westbury with Tack. Paige met the love of her life, Randy Baker. Their relationship was a tumultuous one. Randy was a bonafide bad boy in every sense of the word. By today's standards, he would be called a straight thug. She could not get enough of him and knew she was just one of many. Being young, dumb, and in love, she set out to prove she was more ride or die than any of the others. Young love can be a wondrous thing, but not in this instance. Randy lived by a true bad boy code, and Paige was drawn to it, like a moth to a flame. She found someone who was as dark and jaded as she was. Their relationship was, if nothing else, exciting; and it got her away from all of us.

If you had something Randy wanted, watch out. If he were a character in a movie, he would definitely be Debo from the movie *Friday*.

One day, my friends and I were sitting on the curb playing Jacks I was working on my sixes when Randy rounded the corner of Maplewood Drive onto Holly Lane in Olympic stride. One of New York's finest, nightstick in hand, was in hot pursuit. Though Randy easily had him by a quarter of a block, he stopped and bent over, both hands on his knees, breathing deep. We watched the officer raise the stick with bated breath as he drew near. Randy, still bent, pivoted and came up with a two-punch that rivaled heavyweight champion Floyd Mayweather. The officer never knew what hit him. Now as I write this, I can hear Chris Tucker taunt his famous line in the movie *Friday, "You got knocked the fuck out!"* You remember the scene when Debo knocked out the guy he stole the beach cruiser from. Well, this was no movie, and it did not have a happy ending.

Randy continued to run down Holly Lane and jumped the dead-end fence. My friends and I ran after him to watch what would happen next. The dead-end fence divides Holly Lane, Barn Street, and Park Avenue. By the time we made it to the fence, it was mayhem. Several police officers had him pinned down to the ground. They beat him bloody.

I screamed, "No, stop," and tried to jump the fence.

Randy lay there being beaten, but managed to shriek, "Maggie, go home. Don't watch!" It was at that instance I knew he really cared about Paige. Through his pain, he wanted to keep me safe, if only for her. At seven, there was not anything I could do, except what I knew best. As I ran home to tell Paige what happened, I made eye contact with the injured officer. The expression on his face said it all. "I knew I should have called in sick today!"

Randy's escapades were legendary and did not end there. A few years passed, and I was in middle school. It was lunchtime, and I was outside enjoying the spring air with my friends.

His cousin walked pass me, nonchalantly he said, "Hi, Maggie."

"Hi, George, what are you doing here?"

At the time, I did not give much thought as to why a grown man with no children would be at the middle school. I was also a bit annoyed at how he blew me off in front of my friends.

The bell rang prematurely, as a frantic announcement followed. "All students return to the lunchroom immediately."

Later that evening, I found out that Randy and George robbed the bank down the street from my school. They sought refuge in the crowd of students after the police chased them. Crime does not pay; they were later apprehended. It was discovered that they had been on a robbery spree up and down Long Island.

Randy was the mastermind behind some lucrative capers. He was definitely a career criminal; however, the sad thing about it is he's a smart guy. Every time he went to jail, he would go to the law library and get himself right back out. (His cousin, George, was not as fortunate. He definitely was not the brains of the operation, neither the muscle, nor the lookout for that matter, or the getaway driver, or the person who held the gun, or bag of loot. Truthfully I think he just kept Randy company.) There are hood stars on every corner of every hood! You don't believe me; break down the infrastructure of any drug ring. You will find CEOs, scientist, mathematicians, and an organized hierarchy from captains, lieutenants, to soldiers. Imagine if that negative energy was used for good.

Randy was by all accounts a seventies' Robin Hood. Maybe that is what Paige loved about him. I never saw him turn down a person in need. Unfortunately that noble quality would lead to his downfall. There are times when you have to just say no. Or you will be eaten alive. The one thing I do thank Mother for is all the "isms" she drilled in me. I guess you can call them survival lessons. As crazy as some of them were, they help me survive several baptisms by fire. I wished more of my siblings had paid closer attention at the "school of Hattie Mae" more often. Maybe they would have survived too.

Paige's relationship with Randy was definitely unhealthy for her. She picked the same man as Mother. Someone who could not give her the one thing she deserved. As well as the fact that he also violated several of the major isms! "(1)Self-preservation is key! (2) Never let your left know what your right is doing. (3) Always do your dirt by yourself, Maggie! (4) Come up with your own stupid shit to do. (5) If I'm caught—we *all caught*." Everyone in the neighborhood loved him though, especially Mother. (Birds of a feather . . .)

He did, however, pay attention to one ism: "Technicalities, semantics, the little things, yes all the pieces matter!"

You can say it was dumb luck, but dumb luck or not, just when you wrote him off, I'll be dang if he would not be standing there looking at you. After his arrest, he would get in the law library and get himself out. It seems though that dumb luck or genius ran out because he is doing life in prison for a drug deal gone wrong. Do they usually go any other way? Not where I lived! You know what, never say never. The doorbell could ring, and he could be standing on the step yet again.

By eighteen, Paige dropped out of high school and was in and out of our house like a revolving door. Sometimes we did not see her for weeks, then she would pop up and stay a while, and just like that she was gone again. I fell through the cracks when she was gone. I had no mother figure to guide me, love me, and nurture me. Whichever brother or sister would let me latch on was the one that became my surrogate mother/father. Usually Roddy, but he is only four years older than I am, so what could he really do.

Randy had long moved out of his mother's home because of his poor career choices. His mother, Glenda, did not care for Paige; but she did however love the girl who was the third angle in their on/off again love triangle. Running in circles and triangles ran her down! By twenty, Paige was heavily into the drug scene. It was the ugly eighties, who wasn't? Hell, I smoked so much pot at that time; that one night I was over a friend's house and we were smoking and drinking, I looked in my cup, and there doing the backstroke was the biggest roach. I was so messed up that I flicked his ass out of the cup and kept on drinking. (Yes, I'm gagging as I am telling the story.) Although I was young, I do remember she started to look different. Her once radiant skin was now sallow. She did not keep up on her mani-pedi any longer; she was moody and slept a lot.

When I was twelve, my sister was twenty-four. I broke my left leg. The doctor said that the leg would not continue to grow. So the following year, the doctor surgically broke the right leg so they would both remain the same. I would only continue to grow from the torso up. I endured years of pain due to endless surgeries and rehabilitation. You know that saying "everything happens for a reason." Well, Paige stepped up and took great care of me. Caring for me became her zeal for life. She moved back home, and things were just as I liked them. I had *my* Paige back. It took three years for me to heal and return to school. And just like that, she was gone. She moved to Alabama to get her life back on track. The demons were too strong for her to conquer, and they chased her all the way there. When she returned, she was worse off than before she left.

Now a freshman in high school, I knew a few things; and one of them was that bitch did not look, smell, or act right. At that time, our house was filled to capacity. Lauren left her husband and returned with their two children and was sleeping in the bottom bunk bed in my room. Paige returned home; it was apparent to everyone her demons had taken control of her and were winning. She slept on my bedroom floor on a pallet. Five people in a room the size of a walk-in closet was cramped, even if two of them were toddlers. But we made the best of it. That was something we knew how to do. Making something out of nothing became as easy as breathing air. Not for nothing my siblings and I always came together in a time of need. That is all we knew. We made it one big slumber party especially for the two babies. Those were some of the best times in my life.

One night, Paige and Lauren let me go out with them. I borrowed an outfit from my neighbor Chrissy who was much older than I was, and she curled my hair. She was often called one of the most beautiful girls in Westbury because of her lacquer like skin and hourglass figure. Chrissy made me look like I was at least twenty years old. Being that I was never allowed off our block, not many people other than my siblings' friends knew me. It was graduation night, and parties were everywhere, so we went to the Foreign Legion—a local dive bar/club. More like a hole in the wall. There was only one way in and one way out. It was hot as hell in there. The abundance of products she put in my hair to help it curl started to melt and roll down my neck.

I told Lauren that I would wait outside. This guy followed me outside and started talking to me. Asking me all the stupid questions guys ask when they are trying to get in your pants. What he did not know was I knew him. His name was Franklin, an acquaintance of Lauren's husband, Jake. He did not recognize me for the simple fact that, when guys came around I was always sent out the congregating area. I do not know why exactly, but my brothers never let me be around their male friends. Maybe it was their way of protecting me from the world or because their friends were just plain nasty like them.

I just let him talk, and talk, and talk. In the very least he was a cutie, and it broke up the boredom of standing alone. All right I was flattered that this much older guy was attracted to me. He was shooting all his game, but making no baskets. Then he became a little touchy feely. But I was not complaining. I was pleasantly surprised that I had such an effect on him. Caught up in the moment, I let him stroke the side of my face, run his fingers through my hair, and put his hands on my hips and pull me closer to him. Thank goodness I had eaten like a half of box of Tic Tacs before he approached me. Excitedly I licked my lips, opened my mouth, and closed my eyes in anticipation of what was to come. To this day, I do not know where she appeared from, but when I opened my eyes in disappointment, because of what was supposed to come next did not, Paige had a knife to his throat just before our lips met. I told you before I have a type, and he definitely fit it. The music and those three drinks my neighbor gave me in the bar did not hurt either. "Motherfucker, if you put your hands on her again, you better make sure you enjoy it, because it will be the last time you ever feel anything."

"Paige, what's wrong? Why are you blocking?"

"What's wrong is you out here with your hand all over my fourteen-year-old sister. That's what the fuck is wrong."

Lauren came running outside laughing. "Paige, put that knife down." Now, a crowd of people gathered.

He pleaded, "Lauren, you know I did not do anything. I didn't even know she was your sister. If I had known she was fourteen, I would have never spoken to her. She doesn't look fourteen! How was I supposed to know?" A small trickle of blood flowed down his neck. "Ahh, ask her. I did not do anything." He looked at me. "Come on, Paige, that shit hurts."

"He didn't do anything, I swear. We were just talking."

"Why he had his hands on you then?"

"I was about to tell him who I am. He thought I was new in town."

She took the knife from his throat. "You got to go home, Maggie, before my ass end up in jail tonight."

"Paige, why?"

"Because I said so."

I knew not to ask again.

"Well, I'm not walking her home."

"She can't walk alone, Lauren."

"I'll walk her."

Paige pointed the knife at him.

Lauren laughed. "Don't make me get Jake to kick your ass."

"I am not going do nothing to her. My night is ruined. I'm going home to take a cold shower and put a Band-Aid on my neck."

"You better not touch her."

Lauren snapped, "He's not gonna do nothing to her, go ahead and walk her."

I told them I would wait up for them. The conversation on the way home definitely was not the same as earlier. He was a perfect gentleman. Or scared to death Paige would stick his ass again. "By the way, your breath smells really good!"

"Thank you."

"Good night."

"See ya."

Paige disappeared for longer and longer periods of time and subsequently moved in with her friend Fiona who had about ten children. I have never seen someone with so many kids take such good care of them. One evening, she stopped by. Richard and Brian argued with her in the kitchen. Mother broke up the argument and asked what was going on. Richard told her that Paige was dating a drug dealer named Ruthless. They confronted him, and he told them that although he sold drugs, he never gave her any. The conversation turned violent. Mother jumped on her and beat her within an inch of her life. With the exception of Lauren's two toddlers and me, everyone in the kitchen tried to get Mother off Paige. I stood with the children, the three of us crying. The children were crying because of all the screaming, and me because my hero was actually human after all.

That beat down further strained their relationship. I loathe confrontation, especially when Hattie Mae was/is involved. I told you before Mother is many things, but a punk was never one of them. A few years earlier, my classmates who saw Mother scale a ten-foot fence after running two miles teased me relentlessly. I was the butt of the joke for many years. Cathy, the girl who was the third angle in the infamous love triangle, recruited her aunt who was Mother's age to help her beat up Paige. A neighbor saw what was going on and ran to get Mother. After she scaled the fence, she beat the hell out of the aunt, while Paige excitedly took care of Cathy. It was the principle of the matter. Mother could fuck us up, but you couldn't.

For the most part, Mother was a cool type of mother; she was reasonable and did not rise to every occasion. (By the time I came along, she was just too damn tired to care what I did.) But once you took her there, it was no going back. Hearing something about your daughter from the streets most definitely took Hattie Mae from zero to sixty and back again. Life changed for me that day and Paige too. I began to watch her like a hawk. Although several family members turned their back on her, I felt it was my responsibility to save her. It was my turn to care for her; after all, she had always been there for us. Even for the most provincial things.

Now sixteen, a boy whom I had known almost all my life began to look different to me in the eleventh grade. He had been pursuing me since the ninth grade, but I was not allowed to date. (I wasn't allowed to date in the eleventh grade either, but he fit the type!) One disadvantage about being the youngest child is, everything that your older siblings did, they made it a point not to let you do. Paige, however, intervened on my behalf and convinced Mother to let me date him. She said I was weird enough. Little did she know that it would turn out to be double trouble for her. Her ass thought if I was preoccupied I would leave her alone!

While I was following and watching her every move, James was right at my side helping me. We slow walked her down many nights. She would get so tired of us following her, me crying with snot hanging from my nose, and him arguing with her for making me cry. She would give up her quest for temporary euphoria and go home cursing us out the whole way. I will always love him for that, and I think she does also. James is good and loyal that way! Protecting me and anyone he knows that means something to me. I believe she too saw that quality in him from the day she met him. That he would always take care of me, as she had once done. Unfortunately she is stuck with me, no matter what, and I her. But she didn't have to be bothered with him. Amazingly enough they are very close. No, don't get out the violins; they curse each other out every time they speak. It's the way they communicate, but I dare anyone to touch either, in front of the other, and watch what would happen! She always refers to him as her brother, and she is our children's godmother.

It took many years for her to get herself together. Those damn demons would not let go. With every relapse I was there, especially when other members of our family wanted nothing to do with her. Told her she was not their sister. But not me! To discard her as if she was trash would be like cutting out my heart and throwing it away. I could and would never do that.

She got her shit together after losing a good job though. It was the embarrassment that slapped some sense in her. After working her way to the top (This is where her obsessive-compulsive disorder came in handy), she did something so . . . If stupid was a crime, she would still be locked up. But I guess if it was a crime, I am sure many of us would have a criminal record right along with her. It is actually more comical than criminal. The demon whispering in her ear that she was unworthy got louder and louder. Whispers became screams so loud that she could not hear the praises being sang to her. Self-sabotage was for sale just mere steps outside the doorway. Of course she thought she could control it. Somewhere deep down I knew, but did not want to admit it. It is not rocket science; if nothing else, my sister is consistent.

First she starts with nonalcoholic beer. Next, it is wine coolers by the four packs. Then it is regular beer shortly thereafter. She will start with maybe one or two, next thing you know it will be four and then the whole six-pack. Now we are seriously spiraling out of control. This is where I am watching and waiting for the other shoe to fall, because the next step in the scenario is avoidance. She will avoid me like I have the plague. The funny thing is if I had the plague, that bitch would be the one to take care of me. But she cannot stand to look into my big judgmental eyes. You remember them—they are the same judgmental eyes Mother hated looking at when she drank. The all tell sign is the company she would keep. Everybody was her friend. "They are cool people. Ya'll think ya'll better than everyone else." I know you know that whole song and dance; if you don't, you better take notes. Although addiction is played as a ghetto song, the lyrics and dance moves are the same for whatever the drug of choice may be. There are two more steps before you get your umbrella, folks, because the shit is about to hit the fan.

Slowly but surely, that monkey on her back turned into a gorilla. Now to fully understand this, I hope you are sitting down because this is truly one of the most idiotic things a person could do. Paige worked her way up from fry cook to general manager of a well-known fast-food restaurant. She counted out the money the store had made on a Saturday. It is common sense that the store made more on weekends than on weekdays. She counted out ten thousand dollars. Well, you can see where this is going, but not quite. That bitch stole one hundred dollars. Yes, I said one hundred dollars. She did not even steal the entire ten thousand dollars not even close. That night, it was not all about the Benjamins, just one of them. Moreover, it was not even the new big face Benjamin Franklin. You will never guess what it was for. To go to bingo, yes and B-I-N-G-O was his name oh! Now, please don't get me wrong, I am not condoning what she did because wrong is wrong. No matter how big or how small. You can put lipstick on a pig, yet it is still a pig. Listen, there is one thing you must understand about me. I paid close attention while attending the "school of Hattie Mae." When I fuck up, I fuck up big! I am sorry, but I just do not like little things. If it is little, you better have something extra to go along with it. "First impressions are everything, Maggie, so give it your all. If they are going to talk about you, give them something to talk about. (*SOH* lessons 304 & 305!) Please believe if I am going to go to jail, I'm damn sure not going for penny-andy stuff. It would have been for the whole ten thousand. But that's just me.

Now I must state that my sister was making well over a thousand dollars a week. This was 1994, in North Carolina. There are people who don't make that much today, here in New York. She had no children or real bills except for a few credit cards. Although she put the money back the next day, it was too late. Another ism she didn't listen to: "*When doing dirt, always make sure no one is watching!*" There was a little camera in her office, recording every fart she made, booger she picked, and hundred dollars she stole. I know—crazy! The company did not press charges because she put the money back, but they fired her. The regional manager told her she was the best GM he had to date and was sorry that he had to let her go.

After losing that job, she fell into a deep depression and pulled me in with her. We fell fast and hard. It was a trying time. My emotions were all over the place. I was so focused and consumed with her that I became her. It was to the point I started self-medicating myself. My medicine of choice was Absolute Vodka, and I had many refills. When I ran out, I would drink whatever was available, smoked weed, and took prescription pills telling myself all the while I was numbing her pain. Mother's best friend, Maria, gave me my first Valium in middle school. It wasn't the only thing she gave me; whatever she had, I was privy too. Needless to say, she became my best friend too. I never got into the hard stuff like crack, cocaine, and heroine, or anything like that. (Except for that one time, but that was Lauren's fault.) For one thing, I saw what it did to the people around me, selling and using. The second thing, I hate needles. I just wanted enough of a high to escape the circus going on around me. Little did the ringmaster know, I would become a full-blown alcoholic by twenty years old. Hey, I started drinking at a very early age. Becoming a hoe was never part of the equation. Though one would tend to think that would be part of the progression. Paige would have killed me if she knew that I was drinking at twelve. By the time she did find out, it was too late. She figured as long as she "watched" me, I would be okay. But how can she watch me, and me her, if we both fucked up? We did not do a good job, but damn if we did not have a great time trying.

For four years, I was the party girl of the boondocks. She often told me she was afraid for me because I was traveling down many of the roads she herself once traveled. The only difference was that I was more open to people, where she was paranoid and suspicious, by rights. I welcomed the strange and uninhibited. At that time, I thrived on it. My friends were societal rejects. A cultural underbelly that was looking for many of the same things I was. We filled the gaps in each other's lives. Drug addicts, hoes, alcoholics, gay, straight, bisexual, black and white, the everyday working person looking for some excitement in his/her boring-ass life—it did not matter. If I was not broke as hell, Paris Hilton, Nicole Richie, and Kim Kardashian probably would have been some of my best friends, minus the sex tape of course.

Then again there was that time when Mother went away for a week and left me home alone. The neighbors hated when she was away. Paige lived with her boyfriend in a seedy trailer park across town. It was the type of place you took a chance every time you visited. It did not make a difference if you locked the car doors or not. If something was seen that was wanted, the windows would be busted out to get it, or the whole damn car would be gone before you got a chance to come outside. I decided to throw a pool party. How it got back to Paige I do not know, because she was not going to be invited. It was probably one of my big-mouth friends that told her.

They loved her and often called her for advice. Another thing you must know about Paige (as if I have not told you enough of her business already) is that she knows how to turn something, anything, and everything into something about her.

She called me and said, "I want to come to the party."

"No, Paige, you're not coming, and I am not playing!"

"If you don't let me come, I'm going to call Mother and let her know."

"Who cares, what can she really do? She's a billion miles away. By the time she gets here, it will be long over."

"Well then, I'll call the police and tell them someone has broken into my mother's house."

"You get me sick, you fucking bitch. Don't laugh. You better not act up either, I swear."

What else was I to do? I made her promise that she would not drink. She agreed. I picked them up, and she had a couple of very nice bottles of wine with her that *she said* were for the guest. We made it back to the house. She made some finger foods; I barbequed and turned up the music. Let the party begin! Everyone showed up; it was going great, until.

Like I told you, a party did not start until my girls and I got there and set it off. Especially Lauren and me; but for this extravaganza, she was out of town. No extra set of eyes and hands for that matter where I needed them. Since it was at my house most of the work was done. Paige sat in the kitchen and was actually behaving. Her boyfriend mingled and talked with some of the guys. At the same time as I walked through the kitchen door to check on her, a guest was coming in the back door. As I entered, she glared at me through puckered brows.

"What?"

"What the hell are you doing?"

I stopped dead in my tracks.

Nonchalantly the guy asked, "What's wrong?"

She yelled, "Why the hell are you naked in Mother's kitchen?"

"We need more ice."

"If you don't get the fuck out of here, I promise you I will not be held liable for what I will do to you."

He leisurely turned and walked out the door. Paige and I ran to the back door and looked out. Everybody was naked. Some were in the pool, and the others were mingling.

"What should I do?"

What I failed to state was we lived next door to a man who did not look like us. This was pre-Obama years, with his purple people-eater lips, and he knocked on our door for the smallest infraction. As we heard it, his dislike of everything black began when his only child was caught servicing the biggest, blackest buck she could find in their home. The only thing that saved him from doing time after the neighbor notified the authorities that his daughter was being raped was their relationship was well known in the neighborhood. One neighbor told the investigator when the parents would leave out the front door, he entered the back door! She was shipped off to somewhere far, shortly thereafter. How he tried to sell it as rape was beyond me, unless his daughter was the rapist. She was the one with the mouthful of balls, and he was the one screaming like a bitch.

Paige said, "Go and make sure everything is cool back there. They're not making noise, and they are all grown. Just the same, do a walk-through. But tell them if they need to come in the kitchen, put something on. I cannot believe he had the nerve to come in here with that little-ass dick. I don't know if I got madder at the fact that his dick was that small, or because he opened the refrigerator. Maybe if he trimmed some of that Afro around it, it would look bigger!"

"Okay, shut up please." I was still in panic mode that half the guest had stripped down to nothing in the backyard. If Mother knew that not only was a soft-porn party going on in her backyard, but somebody went into her refrigerator without any clothes on, my ass would have been thrown out on my ear! I knew Paige was going to hold it over my head for forever and a day. I got some ice and did what she said. Everything was fine; no one was tripping.

As I walked around the pool, one of the "club kids" said, "Maggie, take off your clothes and get in. The water is great."

"Maybe in a bit, there are people in the house, and you know Paige."

I was not about to take my clothes off and swim. Although it was pre-hubby and children, and my body was in the best shape of my life, I was, however, extremely body conscious. Always finding something wrong, I was addicted to exercising (not to mention partying) and weighed one hundred and five pounds wet. I ran five miles a day, followed up with laps in the pool until I collapsed. A military wife who was a good friend of Ann's taught aerobics. I was there three to four times a week, as well as taking advantage of the weight room.

Though lean, I saw fat. My stomach was washboard flat, but I saw flab. I never had, according to Kanye West, "An ass that would swallow a G-String"—but I always had two nice "bee stings" that were perky. My bikini game was amazing! Nevertheless, here she was with these two big old saddle bags floating on top of the water as she swam the back stroke inviting me in my pool. I was almost tempted to go get Paige to throw her ass out. She was after all getting too much attention. But Debra was our home girl. Knowing her, she was probably the one who told everyone to take their clothes off.

Deb was probably the one who told Paige about the party. That was the one issue I had with her. She had loose lips, and Paige knew how to get every tidbit of information out of her! Though one of the club kids, Paige did not party with us that often. But Deb kept her well informed about what she missed. We had some good times with Deb. If some of the best times of my life were partying with Paige and Lauren, others were with Debra. She was wild as hell, and the first black girl I knew to rock confetti pink hair. Of course Paige wanted it. That's why we liked her; she too refused to be put in a box. At six feet tall, she probably wouldn't fit. She was also a freak. I didn't judge her though. Who was

I to judge? Lord knows I do not live in a glass house and have my own idiosyncrasies. Don't we all? That was the thing about the group, no one particular person stood out. With the exception of me and Lauren, for whatever reason, however, I was the voice of sanity. Imagine that? Especially for Paige! Lauren and I looked out for every one that hung out with us.

I think that is why Paige liked being with us, because no matter what she did, she was never ostracized. She was the mother to our hodgepodge group. And I was Mother to her. Knowing that there were actually people crazier than she was made her feel safe. The more they tapped into her wealth of knowledge, the more she felt needed. This, in turn, made me feel happy. Something I had yet to experience.

I went back in the house, and Paige was still sitting at the table, though now, she was halfway through the bottle of wine *she said* was for the guest.

I was pissed. "What the hell are you doing?"

"My nerves are bad, and I am just going to have this one glass."

"The bottle is damn near empty. If you start tripping, you're out, Paige. And I mean it." I did not care if she did call the cops. I went downstairs to check on the guest who did not care to skinny dip. We were laughing and talking when this guy I did not know came running down the stairs soaking wet. The only thing I could focus on was his private parts flopping all over the damn place. I was pleasantly surprised, because he was quite short. But, man, was he, let's just say blessed. Then again who thought Ray Jay would be so well-endowed. Oh please, you know you watched the tape too! The first thing that popped in my head was Paige should see *this* guy. I know I was not the only one staring. Even some of the guys I was sitting with had a look on their faces like "I am not standing next to that guy at the urinal." And I didn't blame them.

It took a minute to understand what he was saying, at first I only got "Crazy bitch, knife, and stab, stab."

So I looked up, and the fear in his eyes snapped me out of my "OMG" fog. "I'm sorry. What did you say?"

"There is a crazy bitch in your front yard trying to stab a guy with a big-ass butcher knife."

It didn't register that that crazy bitch could be Paige. I sat there for what seemed like eternity. Then it hit me—Paige, the bottle of wine, and Lord knows what other shit she got hold of. I ran up the stairs, and I don't remember my feet touching one step. At the front door, which is all glass, I saw Paige holding a big butcher knife. She lunged at her boyfriend who by the way had a belt in his hand. Each time she lunged at him, he hit her with the belt. I watched the spectacle for a moment then intervened, because the guest started to come to the front. I got in between the two of them. (Yes, I know it was the dumbest thing I could have done. But at the time it was the only thing I knew to do.)

"What the hell are you doing?"

"I am going to kill this motherfucker."

"What did he do?"

"I came outside, and he was on the side of the house watching those naked bitches in the back."

"I was not watching them. I was standing here talking with some people. She came out and assumed I was watching them. I am just enjoying the party."

The guy he was talking to said, "Yeah, we were just standing here, and she came out and started screaming, and then she went and got a knife."

Why did he say anything?

"Who the fuck asked you to get all up in my business?"

I tried to defuse the situation because I knew where this was coming from. We had been here before. The guests were like "We are out of here." I tried to calm everyone down, but it was to no avail.

"Paige, ya'll have to go home."

"I'm not going home with her. She's going to kill me in my sleep."

"Okay, you can stay here, and I'll drive Paige home." By the time I got my keys, everyone was gone.

In her most pitiful voice, with tears rolling down her face, she said, "I'm sorry I ruined the party. I had a really good time though."

"Bitch, get in the fucking car."

As I'm driving down the street, I look in the rearview mirror, and her boyfriend is running behind the car. I hit the brake.

He tapped on the window. She rolled it down and said, "I can't let her go home upset by herself." He climbed in the backseat, and she closed the door. By the time I dropped them off and return home, it was 6:00 a.m., and yes I had to clean the entire mess that was left by myself.

North Carolina was a magical place and time for all of us. It gave us something none of us ever had—a place to call home. Nobody constantly was telling us "Pack your shit and get the fuck out." It took some getting used to. It may be twisted, but I missed Tack though. It was that Stockholm syndrome coming back to haunt me. Twenty years of living the same thing can have an abnormal effect on anyone. (Even Jaycee Dugard thought her captures cared about her. She sued the state and won twenty million dollars. All I got was a guilt trip and bad memories. I'm just saying!) Whether you lived there or not, Mother's open-door policy extended six states. All were welcomed. You know the saying "If you build it, they will come." Though we did not technically build it, they did come, in droves. During those times, Mother tended to stay in shadow. Her days of leading the infantry were over. What saved me from the party life was Mother's fiftieth birthday party. I had a little bit, well a lot too much to drink. James came to visit from New York to celebrate with us. Let's just say one thing led to another, and the use of generic birth control while drinking was not a good mix. (That's why I beg to differ with anyone who says generic is the same as name brand.) A month later, Paige took me to the doctor because I thought I had the flu. Behold nine months later, a baby girl was born.

Although it was a hell of a party, I was not anticipating on getting a gift as well. I was not capable of being anyone's mother. Mother had to remind me to feed and walk my wirehaired fox terrier, Arrie. Honestly, I did not know what I was going to do! But Paige convinced me that it was time for me to settle down. Because I was on the verge of looking in the mirror and seeing her face staring back at me.

She has a way of convincing people of things. I have learned in my forty-two years of life that she can persuade an Eskimo to buy ice, in winter. She truly has game; she got it from Mother. My so-called friends dropped me because I totally gave up the party life. But my one true friend remained; she was there for me my entire pregnancy. She treated me as if I'm carrying the second coming of Jesus. We were together a lot. I loved it.

After I gave birth, my husband wanted the baby, and I had to move back to New York. It was the most gut-wrenching decision I ever had to make. I was afraid if I left, all hell would break loose.

Mother came to me and said, "You need to give James a chance to do what's right."

"You know what'll happen if I leave."

"Maggie, you cannot save Paige, just as you could not save me."

The first month I was gone, I ran my phone bill up to seven hundred dollars trying to keep track of her. I would go back to North Carolina so much it seemed like I never left. I was living an unrealistic life of wanting to save my sister, being a good wife, and mother to my child. As you know, God has a way of ordering our steps. My daughter became very ill, and we did not know if she would live. She had to take priority. Paige had her trials and tribulations, but she would not have had it any other way. She would have to travel alone and save herself. I could no longer be a passenger on her journey.

Not being able to let go of the past has caused her to think that she has to prove she is better than how she was treated. She has to have more, be more, and do more than anyone else. My sister does not adhere to less is more. She has gone from one extreme to another. Addiction, like the devil, can take many forms; but he is still the devil, thus her addiction is . . .

What Paige often fails to realize is that, sometimes, God will reduce us, to rebuild us up even higher than we ever were. Given that, never to have suffered, would never to have been blessed. And just when you think you'll continue spinning your wheels going left and praying the road is not a dead end, He'll laugh and send you right! Consequently meeting your destiny on the same road you avoided traveling.

One day, she was in the grocery store; an unassuming gentleman stared at her. Not the type she was used to, she kept shopping. Three aisles down, she noticed him again.

Her paranoia kicked in. "I know you're not following me, because I promise you, if you are trying to rob me—?"

It was there, in the feminine products aisle, he said, "God just told me that one day you are going to be my wife!"

"If you don't get your backward crazy country ass out of my face, you gonna wish you had."

Divine intervention intervened. They were married nine years ago. He doesn't smoke, drink, or use any kind of drugs. Not even Tylenol. He is a retired military veteran. He has a son from a previous marriage, and they adopted two children. Yes, he is country as hell, but he spoils her rotten.

Paige traded in her old lifestyle for a minivan and a pain-in-the-ass Pomeranian. (He's so cute though.) At one time Alabama was the furthest she had ever traveled. But he makes a point of taking her on vacation twice a year, both domestic and abroad. She doesn't work, which leaves her far too much time on her hands. Therefore, their house looks like QVC and HSN collided.

Not being able to exorcise her demons has caused her to travel down some god-awful roads. Maybe if someone warned her not to give the devil a ride, because he will eventually want to drive, she would have sped past him. I'm going to keep praying for her to address the past. In order to let it go, she has to tell Mother all the things she told me over French fries. That her life was devastated, due to the negligence and abuse which set her on a path of destruction. The burns she sustained made her feel like a monster, even though she is beautiful. That living in constant fear crippled her as a child, as she protected us. Fearing that deviance was the way one shows their love, causing her to love no one, not even herself. Even though she is the most loving people I know. How angry she is at her for not being there to protect her, though she pretends not to be. That being broken as an adult seduced her into a life of debauchery. Once she says it, and not when she is under the influence, she'll be free! Let go and let God. Because I know through God all things are possible. It will be that day she'll be able to not only forgive Mother, but also realize that she did the best she knew how to do, even if it wasn't good enough, just as I did. That she does not have to live in fear any longer, to love and be loved. Because the right man can make you feel as if nothing else matters.

If she doesn't, every step she makes toward the future will have one strongly planted in the past! Fore, it is through forgiveness we are able to move forward.

KEEP DOING THE RIGHT THING, SISTER. YOU DESERVE ALL THE BLESSINGS THAT ARE COMING TO YOU. WHO LOVES YOU, BITCH?

Dear Richard,
If I could travel back in time,
and know what I know today
I'd travel to the day before you passed away.
If I could travel back in time,
I'd travel to our childhood years
and tell you I love, and comfort you in your time of fear
If I could travel back in time,
and know what I know today
I'd travel to the day before you passed away
If I could travel back in time,
and know what I know today
I'd tell you all the things I never got a chance to say!

The day you left had to be the worst day any of us has experienced to date. I can testify to this with conviction because of first handedly witnessing the aftermath of your absence. Although we have been through many things, we always had each other to cover their link in the chain of support. With you missing, the chain weakened, never to be as strong as it once was. Leaving us exposed and succumbing to defeat many, many time. Which is not an easy thing to accept, going into battle and knowing you do not stand a snowball's chance in hell of coming out the victor. Some of us still attempt to fight the good fight, and some concede defeat before the conflict begins. Thus, causing us all to lose a war we did not start! But we are mere soldiers strategically placed on the front line, waiting to be picked off one by one. Not you though, no matter what, you were always ready, come what may. You thrived on it, which could be one reason why some of us have a defeatism attitude. But those days are long gone never to return. IF I TRAVEL BACK IN TIME, AND KNOW WHAT I KNOW TODAY—

Paige and Richard have the same father and suffered with many of the same issues. Especially that strike before being struck mentality. Richard never got a chance to know his father. When Mother fled, she was pregnant and never told him, especially after he was born. Doctors say that an unborn child experiences everything the mother experiences. If that is truly the case, can they hear the pitch of voices? As well as what the mother eats and drinks all have an effect on the fetus. My brother was doomed from the start.

He grew in the womb of a woman who lived in constant fear; does that mean he would be fearful or feared? He grew in the womb of a woman who was being abused; does he have a greater preponderance to become a victim, or victimizer? He grew in the womb of a woman who abused alcohol; will he also abuse alcohol, or will he abstain? I cannot answer for all the unborn children who grew in these conditions, but I know how these conditions affected my brother.

Richard Allen Koger forever left this world on March 3, 1991. Leaving behind the devastation of a 747 crashing into an empty field, after being hijacked. His hijacker, however, was not someone you can see, feel, or touch; but a disease that left him a shell of the man he once was. He was born with an epileptic disorder he had actually grown out of as a young child. Until one fated day, that only happens to one in a blah, blah, blah chance. You see I am a big believer of destiny and that all things happen for a reason. Good, bad, or otherwise! Whatever that *thing* is supposed to happen, will find a way to manifest no matter what you do. Though there are many paths one can travel, and things may come to pass differently, they will find a way to pass. How you deal with these *manifestations* is what ultimately dictates ones path on this big old rock. Sure you may choose to go left thus deflecting what was to come on the right, but be mindful that something will come.

Manifest your destiny, you fool! See it in your mind's eye, believe it, and go for it! Come what may. I do not believe that there is just one path, but many that intermingle into one another. Like a maze of life you navigate. You may think it is weird, but I told you before, I do not dance to the beat of anyone else's drummer. I make my own beat (in my head, it has a driving pulse, yet smooth and is always uplifting. The genre is a compilation of old school and new school: Tina Marie, Donna Summer, Al Green, the Bee Gees, to Jill Scott, Ledisi, Musiq of course, old school hip hop/ some new but not much, Leela James and a drop of Mary J. Blige, Beyonce, and Alicia Keys. I do however, depending on what and how the day is going, add in a few others. I guess you can call it a mix tape that continuously plays in my *Apple iHead*! You know it's funny.)

Richard was working with my father, Herman, at his construction company. My father was contracted to do some cleanup work after Hurricane Hugo in 1989. Normally Richard did not work for Dad, but he needed the extra help. Although Hurricane Hugo was technically a tropical storm, it wreaked havoc up and down Long Island. The majority of the island experienced power outages. Accompanying the debris was fallen power lines. As he assisted someone removing a tree from the street, he accidentally stepped on a *live* power line. Massive amounts of voltages ran through his body and triggered his epilepsy. The doctors could not explain medically how he survived. But by the grace of God . . .

Shortly thereafter, he began having Grand Mall Seizures. The doctors were not able to get them under control, and his love of beer did not help his condition. Although all seizures are bad, Grand Mall Seizures are the worse. The first couple of times I saw him experience them were scary. He trashed about on the floor from violent muscle contractions and loss of consciousness. After Richard had a seizure, he would not recognize us and hallucinated, which caused him to become violent. Getting him to the hospital for treatment was hell. He usually ended up in the small psychiatric unit of Meadow Brook Hospital.

The doctors tried to regulate him with medication. It seemed to have the opposite effect. He seized so often that he had to go directly to a larger psychiatric hospital which was several miles from our house. Meadowbrook could no longer accommodate his needs. Kings Park Psychiatric Hospital did not provide transportation. You cannot imagine riding with someone who is in a psychotic state, who doesn't know who he is, more or less who you are, and/or where you are taking him. I was forbidden to drive him anywhere for that very reason. Having a need to fix things, I went against what I was told. One day he begged me to please take him to the store. He just had to have a pack of New Ports in the box.

What else could I do? I couldn't tell him no. You see, there is one thing you must know about Richard. He prided himself on never asking anyone for anything! But he would always offer you half of his last. So if he asked you for something, you felt obligated to oblige his request, just because he asked and was sick on top of it.

We got in the car and headed for the store. Well, he must have had a mini seizure along the way because he started talking about hell and demons. As he looked out the window, he pointed out all the devil's advocates walking down the street and driving alongside us. Surfeit to say, I am starting to panic, the people he pointed at were people we knew all our lives. People we went to school with, neighbors, and friends. Although I wasn't seeing what he saw, his fear frightened me. I hit the gas when he turned toward me and started staring at me. What did he see in me?

Although I did not turn to look back at him, I could see him out of my peripheral vision. His expression was not fearful; it was just blank. Was I a demon also? I was not sure if he recognized me or not, so I pretended not to see him. My heart was pounding, as I prayed in my head, “God, please do not let him hit me.” His hands were huge. He lunged for the steering wheel, so I held tight with both hands. I screamed as the car swerved to the right. Just as quick as he lunged for the steering wheel, he fell back in his seat. It was weird, and I cannot fully explain it, but a higher power intervened on my behalf that day.

Unfortunately, we were too far from home to turn around and not yet close enough to the store to seek help. I did the next best thing; I had to find somebody to ride with us. If he went off, somebody else would be in the car to catch that ass whooping other than me. James was always cool with Richard, and we were close to his house. As I entered his house, I fell to my knees and succumbed to my fear. His mother called my house and explained what was going on. My family wanted to come get him, but that would have made it worse.

Although I was afraid, I was more ashamed of the fact that I was afraid of my brother than being afraid. The pain of what he would do would eventually wear off, but shame can last a lifetime. Richard always took his role as oldest brother very seriously. His protective nature is what got him put out of Tack’s house. He looked out for all of us in one form or another. And now I was afraid of him. I told them I would get him home after I got his cigarettes. Yes, I was taking a big chance, but I didn’t care. Come hell, high water, or ass whooping he was going to get those damn cigarettes. So I swallowed my fear.

James and I came out of the house, and he said, “What’s up, Fish? Can I ride with ya’ll to the store?”

“It ain’t my car!”

"Well, do you mind if I sit in the front with Maggie?"

Richard got out the car, and James held the seat up for him. He squeezed his six foot five frame in the backseat of my small two-door Chevy Geo Storm. I prayed the whole way as James made small talk with him. The apprehension of sitting in front of my brother was apparent. Richard's conversation turned to God, heaven, angels, and the apostles.

The last thing he said before we pulled in the driveway was, "Yo, Jay, if you want me to iron your clothes for work next week, bring 'em by early."

When we pulled up, the whole family was there waiting. It was horrible. He may not have recognized us, but he damn sure knew when he was on his way to that hospital and would beat the hell out of us the whole way there. Brian and Roderick got the brunt of it because they told the rest of us to get back. Once there, the orderlies would come out and get him which was even more heart wrenching to watch. I always turned my back and put my hand over my ears to drown out his screams of being captured by the devil's minions and/or monsters.

Richard left behind two young daughters, now grown women. He loved them dearly. One day his daughter Channel came to visit him as she often did. Those visits were the highlight of his day. I do not think he was so much a good boyfriend because he had a lot of nice girlfriends that we all hoped he would settle down with, but he most definitely was a great father. I am talking about the kind of father that made sure his daughter's hair was combed and her clothing was neat before they went out. Channel was a daddy's girl without question.

He decided to take her for a walk before she went home. It was a beautiful day, and he had not seized in a couple of weeks. But he was still reminded not to go far and especially not to go down any back roads. Channel was about three or four at the time. As they attempted to cross the street, he had a seizure and collapsed on Prospect and Urban Avenue, a four-lane high-traffic street. The one good thing about a small town is everyone knows everyone. Peter, Chrissy's brother, ran to our house and informed us what happened. He said that Richard tried to drag himself back on the curb. But could not and held on to his little girl's hand as long as he could, until he actually hit the ground. What amazed the onlookers, however, was first Channel stretched out her little hand to stop the oncoming traffic as he lay in the street. She then sat down and put his head in her lap and kept it from hitting the ground. As he thrashed about, she continued to protect him and would not let anyone touch him. When we arrived, she was still screaming to get away from her daddy. The look on her face was sheer terror, as she held on to him for dear life. Children are so much smarter than we give them credit for.

By this point, Richard lived with Roderick and his girlfriend, Valerie. Brian and Roderick did their best to care for him, making sure he not only had his medication, but also took it. They tried to stop him from drinking beer and eat healthier. The last time I saw Richard was after he had a seizure and could not talk or eat due to his teeth slicing and puncturing his tongue. It was severely swollen. I went to spend a little time with him and take him some cigarettes and ice cream. The following week, he was gone.

Richard's relationship with Mother was a protective one. He always came to her rescue. Which is what led to in my opinion his buck of anything authorities. I mean if you are protecting the person who is supposed to be protecting you, what does that leave. He did not get along with our stepfather, Tack, at all. I think Tack was afraid of him. When Mother and Tack argued, Richard would get in his face. Richard assaulted Tack in her defense. Tack said that he could no longer live at the house. His ultimatum at gunpoint "Either he goes or you all go" led to his sacrifice to save the rest of us. That guilt ate at us all, especially Mother. The first few days he stayed with some friends. But he soon wore out his welcome. We would sneak him in to eat and sleep on the floor after Tack went to bed. When he went to work, Richard was able to come out of hiding. This went on for a few years.

Although trouble seemed to follow him, he was an overall sweet person and definitely misunderstood. That was one of the main things that got him into trouble. People did not seem to understand him. He just wanted to belong. But a free spirit can neither be controlled, nor confined. He hung with a medley of friends that I guess wanted to belong to something as well. If they were a click in high school, they would have been the "others." When I think of them, I think of Bill Cosby's *The Fat Albert Gang*. If you lived under a rock for the past thirty years and have not heard of it, it was a popular Saturday-morning cartoon about an African-American boy named Fat Albert and his mishmash of friends. The show carried a positive message or morality as the kids got into and out of various kinds of mischief. In my mind, Richard was Fat Albert, albeit he was not fat "Hey, hey, hey." Stanley, his ace, was Rudy. He was the quiet type, tall, lanky, and unpretentious.

They were the type that snubbed their noses at authority and refused to be assimilated into a societal herd mentality. What's funny is he did not care what people thought of him, except Mother and Paige. Paige had this strange hold on him; I think it was because they had the same father. My brothers and sisters and I were teased a lot for Richard's forward way of thinking. We were all at New Cassel Park one day. Paige, Lauren, and Brian were in the handball court; and I was playing on the playground. It was nothing new for Richard to have arm candy in his company. This one in particular was nothing less than a dime piece that caught the attention of everyone there. Which was not actually a good thing because as drop-dead gorgeous as she was, she was in all intent and purposes a he. To look at her you would never have known, but to look at her "girls" made the invisible obvious. You have to remember this was the early 1980s; there was no such thing as gay marriage; the gay pride parade was not the fabulous extravaganza it is today; *RuPaul's Drag Race*—no, honey, not even thought of. If it was, it was not pitched before the Logo television executives (I love that show) as we know it today.

Just gay bashing, and if you were on the down low, you prayed no one down there with you pushed you out of the closet you were hiding in. But not Richard, he was never good at hide—and-seek. He never fit the boxes people tried to put him in. We accepted him for who he was, which if you must put a label on him today, I guess he would be considered bisexual. Not everyone was so tolerant though. That evening, a crowd of people had gathered in front of our house. They had Richard surrounded tormenting him. As I told you before, you mess with one, you mess with all. Before you knew it, it had become a free-for-all. Two of my sisters were in trenched in the mayhem, one almost lost her freedom and the other one almost lost her life over intolerance.

Ann was stabbed by someone from the mob in the back with an ice pick. The doctors said it was within an inch of her heart. Lauren cut a schoolmate of hers from his collarbone to his navel with a butcher knife. A cut so deep that it took a massive amount of stitches to close and left a scar that would last him a lifetime. His mother and ours were good friends even after the incident.

Hell, I walked their dog, a beautiful collie that looked just like Lassie. His mother refused to press charges or let him tell the authorities who cut him. Richard was sent to Alabama to stay with Grandma Lily until things settled down. He had to go stay with her a lot, and each time he would subsequently run away and hitchhike home.

He was tall, dark, and handsome and loved to dress up. This may seem weird, but his favorite pastime hobby was ironing. It relaxed him, I think. His clothes always looked like he just picked them up from the dry cleaners. People from the neighborhood paid him to iron their clothes, which was how he managed to stay up on the latest fashion trends. His five-finger discount did not hurt either. Hell, James dropped off his clothes every Saturday in order to have them back for school and work the following week.

Richard's teeth eroded to shards of rotten decay due to medication and his insane candy habit. He had a sugar addiction that would rival a heroin addict. I can remember one time Richard came running in the house at top speed. It was in the 1970s. He ran passed everyone sitting in the kitchen. I cannot remember who all the people were, but I do remember Mother and myself were like . . . About two or three minutes later, there was a knock at the door; it was one of our neighbors.

She said, "Hattie Mae, I do not mean to bother you, but Richard was at my house with my kids. When I went into the kitchen, he was in there eating my sugar out of the bowl with his hands. When I told him I was coming over here to let you know what he did, he ran off."

My mother stuck her hand down into her bosom and took out some money and gave it to her. The neighbor continued, "I told him that if he wanted to continue to play with my kids, he couldn't be doing things like that."

Mother apologized about ten times. The straw that broke the camel's back, however, was when the neighbor said, "I do not think it is good for you to let him have that much sweet stuff. He already look like he has problems with his teeth."

"First of all, I do not give my children sugar. That is why he was stealing yours, and second of all, his teeth are like that because he has a medical condition. Every time I try to take him to the dentist, he runs away. I even got him to the door once and he bolted. He did not come home for three days. Maggie, show this bitch your teeth! I try to get that boy to do better, but he just got the devil in him. Now I paid you for the sugar, if you choose not to let him come back to your house, then fuck you! I will understand, and ain't no hard feelings. But do not try to act like them bad ass kids of yours don't do shit. As many times as Richard saved them, when they was getting their asses kicked for stealing all those bicycles. I cannot believe you even knocked on my door with this bullshit. Now have a good day, and I will talk to you later. I got to go tear his ass up!" She ushered her out the door, and that was my cue to disappear.

As a matter of fact, everyone who was in the kitchen dispersed. The worst thing you could do is let someone tell Hattie Mae something you should have told her first. She never liked anyone in her business, because she had a lot of secrets that could not get out. Being "the keeper of secrets," I knew most of them. I learned early (that fourth-grade ass whooping was an Ivy League education) if you came clean with whatever it was you did, your sentence would probably be lighter. You would still have to be punished of course. But Lord help you if you did not, and he never did.

Richard was one of those free spirits that blessed us with his presence way too short. While here though he kicked ass, took names later, and apologized to no one. He lived his life by his own accord, never intending to trespass against anyone and forgiving those who trespassed against him. I believe that he was at peace with his maker.

Mother did not run a religious household by any stretch of the imagination. She sent us to church with anyone who went, which was not regular. All that said by the time of his death what we thought were Richard's hallucinations was in fact his journey of getting on the right path. He quoted verses and passages from the Bible verbatim. He spoke of things that left those he spoke dumbfounded. In hindsight, I truly believe they were not hallucinations at all.

Today would have been his fifty-first birthday (3/2/1960-3/2/2011). *If I could travel back in time, and know what I know today . . .*

Death Does Not Become Her

First, let me apologize that I did not have the courage to tell all of you the things I wanted to tell you when I was living amongst you in the world. I had a problem with showing, or even sharing my emotions—that is face-to-face. It is funny though, this death thing is not as I feared and/or imagined! As I lay here I have to admit, it is not as scary as I thought it would be. Too much television, I guess. The worst part would have to be not being with all of you as I once have. However, I now realize I have been dying a slow death for years. Then I did not know that I should have cherished every passing year, day, and moment. For with them went pieces of my dying self. Memories, both good and bad, however, never die. Take solace in them, in that way our time together will live forever!

I was on a journey of self-discovery, and I needed to know where the cycle of dysfunction in my family began and why. In addition to looking back and learning the causes of why Mother did the things she did to herself. I in turn educated myself with the origins of abuse, I not only sustained at her hands, but also was perpetuating. In an attempt to break a chain that added stronger links with every new generation.

Unfortunately, I was only able to talk about the abuse Mother endured at the hands of her mother, the men in her life, her alcoholism, and the toil it took on her and me. Knowing that that was not all of it! I was not ready or able to talk about what it did to my brothers and sisters. It hurt too much. I knew if I said it out loud, it was true. For years, I believed that if I did not acknowledge it, it did not exist. But it did and needed to be said. Out loud, no longer kept quietly tucked away in my big pumpkin head, driving me crazy. I am releasing it on the wind. I said before if it were not for them, I would not be here to tell you these crazy stories of mine.

At an early age, I knew good things did not happen to everyone, because Mother told me damn near every day. She was shattered in a million pieces. It caused her to become devoid of human compassion, and my siblings and I endured a childhood of trying to put those pieces back together the best we could. But it was never good enough. Her detachment affected each of us differently. I lived by the question: am I my brother's keeper? My answer was always yes, I am, because she told me it had to be. I am the youngest of seven children. I know I stand on the shoulders of giants, who always propelled me toward the sky as their legs shook beneath them, ever pushing me to the stars; but I jumped down and fell to earth, afraid to soar in fear of leaving them. But by trying to help them with their problems, I never addressed my own issues.

Now I realize that there comes a time when you have to cut the strings, although it is forty-plus years after the fact. I had to just let go and let God! I learned the hard way that you cannot live another person's life, because the good you try to do is not necessarily always good for you. Yet there I was. We all were. Together, too close, it was all we knew. We were each other's buoy in the rough sea of life, futilely trying to stay afloat, amidst the ever-knocking waves against our inadequate life preservers, holding on to one another, dearly afraid to let go, because we knew the outcome. Okay, maybe not death, but certainly separation which in turn would mean the same.

Ann,

Mother raised us to defend a sibling in need no matter what. To be by their side, and have no doubt, that in return one would be equally defended. I have never doubted your allegiance to the family, because I have seen you go bare knuckle in defense of . . . But I have doubted your allegiance to me.

It is ironic, your inability to say a civil word to another. It is weird though, because you are the only person in the family with this defective trait. What is ironic however is that there was a time in which you were my superhero—a time when Santa Claus and the tooth fairy was real?

In order to understand this, I have looked many times at the nature of our relationship. Brothers and sisters cannot help but compare themselves to each other. Routinely scrutinizing the talents one will have over the other because we are equally talented in our own way.

This may have been threatening to you, but I was never the enemy and neither were they. We all stood shoulder to shoulder, deep in the trenches of life, in a phalanx like formation—standing, inching forward, closely together as a unit, deployed to fight the good fight. Not knowing who was the actual enemy and not turn on each other. Trying to survive a war in which we did not enlist, but were drafted.

I'm Watching All My Pennies-

Ann is one of those people who strives to do everything the right way. Of all Mother's children, she is probably the most different. If it was not for the fact that she looks like a dark-skinned version of Mother (minus the big-ass glasses) and has her monster booty, I would send them to *The Maury Povich Show* for a maternity test.

My sister is self-determined, independent, self-motivated, and extremely intelligent. Yes, I know we should all be so blessed. Not to say Mother does not possess those same qualities, but just not in a structured productive-citizen type of way. However, these *blessings* per se were nurtured out of something ignominious. Her intent not to follow in Mother's footstep created a very sad little girl. Who not only devised a plan but implemented it, all because she did not want to be like Mother. None of us did, well, except Lauren. Mother is her American idol. Ann was never outwardly emotional. Unfortunately for her, she did not get one iota of Mother's social graces. She is socially inept. My guess is she was so focused on achieving and working her way out of madness; she had little time to learn how to cultivate personal relationships with anyone other than Lauren. And unlike Paige who lashed out at the world, Ann pushed her anger and dismay down, way down. She let it fuel her in other ways. Overachieving! Her past ultimately caught up to her though and took its toll. Little did she know it had been traveling with her all along! Like Paige, she could not let go of the hopes and dreams she wanted the past to be. So her anger replayed like a broken record, over and over again. No matter how short-lived her meritorious glories, they slowly replaced human contact. Accolades cleansed her world of the embarrassment she felt being associated with mediocrity. Achieving was her way out of and also controlling her environment. Her enmity festered like an open wound. In her case, the one who yelled the loudest was not the one who needed to be held and told I love you the most. It was actually the one who was the quietest.

Ann graduated from high school at the top of her class at sixteen years old. Mother said, from the time she was born she was planning her escape. By the age of three, she was reading entire books and doing math. Several colleges offered her scholarships, but escape from the crazy house was a dream deferred. Mother felt that she was too young to fly over the cuckoo's nest. But she could damn well live in it.

Suffice it to say, she does not have many friends, though she has made many acquaintances. Like Mother's, the ones she did have were users. Of all the brothers and sisters, she is the only one to have her own father. I am not sure if he was any better than the other baby daddies. He was never there for her during the time she needed him most, even though his family adored her. She spent summers at her grandmother, Mommy Seal's and Pop-Pop's house.

When Ann returned, she told me stories about her times there. As I listened to her narratives, I imagined that Mommy Seal was a storybook grandmother. I pictured her as somewhat plump with salt-and-pepper hair that was always pinned up. Her caramel-colored skin was complimented by the large round tortoise-shell glasses hanging around her neck from a mother of pearl chain. In this fictitious allegory, she always smelled of fresh-baked pastries and wore an apron that had a light dusting of flour on it. Ann would run up to Mommy Seal and stick her hand in the apron pocket. Magically she pulled fresh-baked cookies out and wash them down, with a cold glass of milk. As Mommy Seal looked down at her with smiling eyes, and stroked her hair.

Hey what do you expect, I was only a kid. I yearned for that type of stuff. Yeah, sure I had Grandma Lily, but it wasn't the same. As Ann learned to bake pastries in her matching apron, I was in hot-ass Alabama learning how to catch a farm-raised chicken for dinner; ring its neck, let it go, and watch it dance the bobble head dance of death; cut its head off and hang it upside down to bleed it; clean the entrails; dip it in hot boiling water *because* "it makes the feathers easier to pluck, lil Maggie"; then cook to your liking. Every bite I swallowed, I puked back up in my mouth, and then swallow it back down. Believe me, the alternative was far worse! Farm fresh my foot. I like buying my chicken from the grocery store wrapped in plastic. I'm sure Ann enjoyed eating the product of her labor, but the not-so funny thing is, after my lesson, I did not eat chicken for a really long time.

When she returned home, she never spoke of her father, Henry. I am not sure what role he played in her life when she visited his mother. Maybe like my father, he ignored her and paid her to sit quietly until the visit was over. For her sake, I hope not. Her father remarried and had three children that do not consider her their sister. I am sure it did not matter to her. She grew up with us, and I myself often questioned, is this bitch really our sister? It was the way she treated us, mostly me. Ann did not put a cutesy little term to it like half sister, quarter, or nothing for her father's children. Like Lauren, Brian, Roddy, and I did for our father's children. They were her father's other children, and that was it.

After she graduated from the local two-year college, she was offered a partial scholarship to a four-year institution. It is in my opinion where the division between her and Mother widened. There was always an underlying rift between them. Ann never accepted the fact that Mother sold herself. Even if it was to her benefit, she just did not buy Mother's old adage that the ends justify the means. Anytime it is brought up, she flees. It caused her to run far and fast. But she could not escape it. She wore Mother's shame like a grimy trench coat. In her mind, when people looked at her, they saw Mother's scarlet letter.

More accolades, and overachieving, caused that festering wound to ooze. Everyone knows however that if you are not enough without them, you will never be enough with them. While attending college, she enrolled in the military Reserves Officers' Training Corps (ROTC) which gave her the stability she longed for. She graduated as the youngest first lieutenant in history. At that time, her father was a drill sergeant in the army. What better way to flatter him than to imitate his line of work, right? Doctors and lawyers descend from legacies. Hell, my gynecologist told me he became a gynecologist because his father was one. He told me the story of how at ten years old his father made him come to work with him every Saturday to learn. While he examined his patients, he said his father explained everything he did, as he smoked a cigarette. He said as he stood shoulder to shoulder beside him, he prayed to God, "Please do not to let his ashes fall in that hole." My daughter's orthodontist was given his first office by his father as soon as he graduated from dental college.

In Ann's case however, it was, at that time, her way to say screw you, asshole. Here are two middle fingers, one up your ass, and the other in your eye. She did it without ever opening her mouth. She did his job better than he did, received accolade after accolade, and promotion after promotion in the process. But the ultimate *coup de grace* would have to be tracking him down at his job and making him salute her in front of all of his coworkers and men under his command. Afterward she turned and leisurely walked away.

Yes, it takes a cold-hearted bitch to do such a thing, but in that instance revenge was a dish best served cold! I wish I had the nerve to do something like that. You know why, because if there is one young man on the cusp of fatherhood who witnessed what she did, maybe he will think twice before he just disregard the seed he planted. One just never knows what that seed will grow into. Yes, there is a 50% chance that it could be a weed, but there is also a 50% chance it could be a rose, tulip, or lily. With a little nurturing applied to nature, there will be more of the latter especially in the minority community.

I get so pissed off when a person of color in politics, sports, or entertainment arenas gets in trouble; and it is splashed all over the news constantly. I do not get mad at the person, but the fact that this person has been made into this contrived angelic persona non grata that holds the aspirations for all little black children. We spend too much time looking outward instead of looking inward. The first thing that is going to be splashed across the headlines is he/she grew up in a single-parent home. His/her father was nowhere to be found! Come on, at some point you have to just get over it and move on. I tricked myself in doing so by constantly telling myself *his fucking lost*, and if I do not do something with myself *he wins*! Sorry, not in this story. Although Charlie Sheen is crazy as hell, I love when he says *winning*! Albeit you cannot make your whole life about winning or you have to continuously keep winning to feel validated. You know it is when you cannot move past something, no matter how blessed you are, that one becomes stuck in the past. You cannot live in the past. Growth in any form becomes arrested. Therefore, atrophy occurs.

It is a shame when the news rebroadcast the story to death and will state another role model falls. That is the problem right there. Just because a person is gifted for what he does, does not automatically make him anointed by God to lead the people. Our problem is we put people on pedestals just to knock them off. Could it be that that person was just a fucked-up individual? Even if his/her father was a dead beat! There are no role models on TV, or magazines, and not on the radio; but there may be role models living in your very own house. To me, role models are those who loved or nurture you from conception. Therefore, be careful of whom you discard.

In Ann's case, Henry was not the only obstacle she had to hurdle. Mother, in her mind, was the biggest impediment of her quest for the gold. It was all her nonsense as a whole. Henry was just one broken rung in her metaphoric ladder to success. Only in her mind, for every two steps she took up, she was knocked back down one. What she failed to realize was that life knocks us all down. However, we have the choice if we are going to get back up. If you make that choice, to stand tall against the wind, it means you are able to see the possibilities of what is to be through the darkness of the clouds of what was. Unfortunately for her, she was not born with a silver spoon in her mouth. Her legacy did not get her in the school she attended. Old-fashioned hard work, sweat, and tears did.

At least she was able to check out for a while. Those of us left behind watched as Mother slid down a razor blade into the bottom of a vodka bottle over and over again. She drowned her shame in a mind-numbing sedation that only soothed her pain and was the accelerant to ours. Ann was truly the blessed one. How much so, I do not believe she truly realized. But with each visit home, she had to have some sort of inkling. Even though we were the New Cassel hillbillies, no one ever realized it at her events. We attended every military or academic event she had, and believe me there were many. I was constantly reminded to be on my best behavior. That, however, depended on which of my brothers and sisters attended. If it was Lauren, I had an endless supply of cocktails; if it was Brian, well, let's just say, "Puff, puff, pass. Craig, you're fucking up the rotation!" I love that movie. What? I didn't inhale!

Case in point: A celebration at the Nassau Coliseum was held to welcome home the Desert Storm veterans. Before the event, the town of New Cassel threw Ann a homecoming parade. Her family was supposed to walk behind her as she sat on top of a car and waved. I was so hung over from going out with Lauren I had to keep sitting on the curb. Once I even lay down. Lauren had to keep picking me up and carrying me along. The problem arose, however, the night before when she knocked on my door. I knew I should have pretended not to be there. Lauren had this weird way of bringing out the worst in me. She convinced me to go to this hole-in-the-wall club where her friend was the bartender. We had all the free drinks we wanted and then came the shootout. After that, my nerves were shot. I needed those drinks to calm me down. (To find out what happened at the club, keep reading.) By the time we made it to the Nassau Coliseum, I passed out at the table and missed the entire ceremony.

I am not sure if by dragging me along was Mother's way of trying to show me what I too could achieve, or if the other brothers and sisters would not watch me. It got to the point where she put me on the Greyhound bus to attend an event. If she did not attend, she would put one of her famous guilt trips on me. In her words, "Someone had to be there to represent the family."

"Someone had to . . ." usually meant me constantly having had to write and visit her. I wore the same blue pinstriped pantsuit with a white ruffled shirt to every event. By the time that suit retired, it walked to its own funeral and lay down in the grave. In the beginning, I rather enjoyed writing and sending/receiving mail to and from all those different countries. But happiness soon became dread; each letter came with a critique and or criticism. You write too big, or not enough, or blah, blah, blah. Slowly but surely a wedge grew between us. Now I know it was not because of all the reasons I told myself. It was because she saw me sloshing down that slippery slope of a road I was traveling. This path of destruction was actually a cry for help that fell on her deaf ears. At that time, I did not want to heed her warnings anyway. They felt like it was just another man down, and she had to keep moving. Now as an adult, I can admit I was jealous she had the courage to do what I did not. Mother and everyone always made such a big deal of her, but just her. Nothing the rest of us did was recognized, unless it was debauchery. At the same time I idolized that she got the hell out. Is that possible?

I remember one time I was about fifteen years old riding the Greyhound bus to Maryland. The ride was long, hot, and funky. By the time I arrived in Maryland, I was sick as a dog and could not even attend the event. That was the last time I was quilted into attending anything for a long time.

Ann did not want to live on campus. So Mother got a job at a local factory to pay the rent for her to live in a studio apartment. She also bought her a car. For our family, Ann was the great black hope. She was the first high school graduate in the family and also the first to voluntarily leave the nest and attend college. The bad thing is you would think that she would make a few steps and reach back to help pull up the next person. Then that person could reach back. No, she was not obligated to help others. Not to say if she had, that any of our lives would have gone in a different direction, who knows? Everything happens for a reason. She could have mentored and bestowed her wisdom though.

She says especially when she is angry how everything falls on her. When she was around the immediate family, she would put up her defenses. As well as talking condescendingly to everyone. I think it was because she expected someone to ask her for something. To tell you the truth, I don't recall any of us asking her for anything. You could barely say hello to her before your head was bitten off. With the exception of Lauren, she needed a place to live with her two children. Her relationship with Lauren's young children turned out to be more than she bargained for. Let's just say children do not forget!

Just about everything I got from her, which wasn't much was made to pay back with interest. If it was not a loan, it was used, and I am not talking about lovingly. For my birthday one year, a package came in the mail. I was very excited because at that time my husband and I were quietly having money issues. When I say quietly, I mean we did not tell anyone. Okay, loudly we were broke. We were drowning in our daughter's medical bills. (For your information, a money issue is usually a code for we were broke as hell.) Our refrigerator was so empty a friend of ours asked us if we turned vegetarian. It was so bad that I would scam fast-food restaurants out of food. It went like this. I would order food at the drive-through. Then go home and call the manager and complain about the food. The restaurant would comp me food, so later in the week I would go back and claim the meals. In between those days, I would go shopping at my in-laws' house. I took my own bags and everything.

Now, you can understand when this package arrived, I was like a kid in a candy store. If you could have been there to see the look on James's face when I opened the box, you would still be laughing. What you have to understand about him is he is one of those people who have a larger-than-life personality. He does not have filters. If you have a booger in your nose, he will tell you, even if he does not know you. You know the type; he is that guy who always comes back with a remark that pisses you off. It comes from a very honest place. (I still keep one eye on him though, I told you one just never knows.) Anyway, in the box was a pair of stinky old tennis sneakers. Well, they were not actually stinky, but they damn sure looked like they smelled.

If the old adage "It's the thought that counts" is true, what did that mean? I really believe she gave me things or loaned me things to provoke a reaction. Lauren always got trips to Vegas or Aruba and whatnots. Hell, that bitch just got a four-bedroom house! I always give good gifts for birthdays and occasions. Even if I just show up at your house, I never come empty-handed. And you dang sure will not leave my house without something. She wanted me to react negatively so she could lecture or be condescending. But I never rose to the occasion. I appreciated when I was in need, she was there. The difference between us is that when I am there for a person, I am there in silence. It was told to me by someone (Mother) that Ann let a lot people con her out of money, which is why she thinks everyone is out to get her. Why we were lumped in that equation, I have no idea! That could be the reason why she equates money with dominance. She uses it as a tool of control, which never works.

When Richard died, Ann was in Saudi Arabia. It was probably the first time I saw her with her defenses down. In a time of tragedy such as this, one's true self tends to come out. It is like that old saying,

"A drunken heart speaks a sober mind." I watched how each of my siblings dealt with their grief. I did not know how to deal with my own, so I buried it deep inside. For the first time in a long time, I felt sorry for her. She became human to me again. Her despair reminded me of the sister I once worshiped.

After she was located in the field, she was told the commanding officer needed to speak with her. When she asked why, she was told that they were not at liberty to say. From what I understand, you are only retrieved from the field when someone in your family has died or in the process of dying. I am not sure how long she had to travel back to base, but it had to be one of the longest rides of her life.

The other would have to be traveling from Saudi Arabia to the United States to attend our twenty-nine-year-old brother's funeral. She was told there was a death in the family; when she asked whom, all she was told was your brother. When she asked, "Which one? I have three," she was told they did not know. It was a few days before she found out. Not knowing who, what, why, or how did something to her. By the time she made it home, she was broken. At a time we should have bonded together, we argued about everything and nothing.

In the beginning of her academic career, I must say she was very nice to me. She came home for vacation, and we would catch the train to New York City. We walked around and ate dirty-water hotdogs from the vending carts and monster pretzels. She gave money to as many homeless people as her budget allowed. I thought she came home just to be with me. But as she began to make more and more "friends," she would invite them to come with us. Eventually I was just there playing a role in her make-believe world to impress her friends. After they left, I became enemy number one again along with everyone else in our uneducated dysfunctional family. She began to come home less and less. Her unemotional abyss got deeper and deeper as her ego got bigger and bigger. Eventually she was no longer from New Cassel; she was from the Hamptons.

I wonder if her stuck-up educated friends knew she not only conspired, but also attempted to kill Grandmother Lily. It was the summer of 1976. Every summer, Mother sent a variation of Ann, Lauren, Brian, Roddy, my cousin little Lauren, and I to visit Grandmother in Greenville, Alabama, so she could rest. Not everyone went every summer. Paige never went. Richard lived there on and off. It was a long hot summer that everyone was ready to come to an end. Mother contacted Grandmother Lily and told her to send us home so we can get ready for school. But Grandmother Lily decided that she was not going to send us home because she could do a better job of raising us.

She stopped accepting calls from Mother and would not let us speak to her. Grandmother went so far as to tell us that Mother gave us to her because she did not want us anymore. We were not allowed to leave the property. A few weeks past, and one day she finally left us alone at the house because she needed to go to town. We ran to a neighbor's house and begged to use the phone. There was no answer, so Ann left a message about what we were told and went back to the house. After dinner, Grandmother Lily asked Lauren if we had left the property. She said no. Although I knew I should have answered no when she asked me, I said yes, we wanted to ask Mother why she did not love us anymore. Everyone except me was beaten within an inch of their lives. The next day we were outside when, and I am not sure who, but someone said as a joke that the only way we were going to get home was over Grandmother Lily's dead body.

That joke sparked a thought. A thought became a plan. Have you heard that the tongue is very powerful and that you can speak things into existence? That is why you have to be very careful of what you say! On the planning day, I was outside with Granddaddy. We were feeding the ducks he bought me. I went inside, and I overheard the plan to kill Grandmother, steal her car, and drive home. There were two problems. One, none of us could legally drive, and two, we had no money for gas, tolls, and food. However, where there is a will, there is a way. The plan unfolded like this. Richard would hit Grandmother Lily in the head with a cinderblock and kill her. After, they would steal her nineteen whatever jalopy, and Ann would drive us back to New York, praying the whole way it did not break down. If stopped by the police, we would plead our case.

Problem one solved! The money issue proved to be more taxing than they anticipated. We knew Grandmother detested banks, so she hid money somewhere on the property, but where? That job was assigned to Lauren. I truly believe Lauren is the manifestation of all the things Ann wants to do and say, and that is why they get along so well. But Ann is too high flatulent. Over the next couple of days, Lauren shadowed Grandmother's every step. She reported back that the money was hid under the third shingle on the sloping side of the roof. Problem two solved! On the day in question, the plan took a turn no one saw coming. Our grandfather did not go to work, and the original plan did not entail leaving any witnesses. When I heard this, I pleaded his case as only a seven-year-old could. "Please don't kill him. I like him. He's nice! If you kill him who will take care of my ducks?"

It was not exactly Johnny Cochran, but it worked. I was to take him outside and keep him busy during the dastardly deed. Ann gave the signal that Grandmother Lily was going to take her afternoon nap. I went outside with Granddaddy, and Richard got the cinderblock. Ann started packing the car, and Lauren ran to get the money. What came next is where the plan turned left! We heard a loud thud, more like three of them, and a howl that came from the bowels of hell. Richard ran out of the house and kept on running. I remember watching and thinking, "Wow, he has a great stride. He should run in the Olympics."

Granddaddy asked, "Why is everybody running 'round like chickens with their heads cut off, little Maggie?"

"Oh, they just killed Grandmother so we can go home." He looked at me as if I had a third eye on my forehead.

His mouth gaped, but before he could say anything, Grandmother stumbled to the door and fell to the ground. "Jimmy, those damn kids tried to kill me." I watched as each droplet of blood dripped to the ground and quickly made a puddle. Lauren rounded the corner and skidded to a stop. Dust plumed around her. Her eyes bulged, and then she turned and hurriedly ran in the direction from which she came. As Ann ran from the other side of the house, her arms full of supplies and bags, she yelled, "Lauren, where are you going?" She must have caught a glimpse of Grandmother on her left, crouching on all fours like a wounded animal. She dropped everything and ran in the opposite direction.

Granddaddy was in shock. "Jimmy, don't just stand there. Help me, I have blood in my eyes." He waddled over to her and helped her up. They struggled to the well where he drew a bucket of water.

"Maggie!" she yelled. "Get over here."

My tiny voice trembled! "Yes, Grandmother?"

"What is going on?"

"I don't know." Granddaddy looked at me. "Well, you would not let us go home." She snatched me, my legs dangled above the ground. "Who hit me with that cinderblock?"

"I . . . I . . . I . . . Ahhhh, you're hurting me." Vomit exploded out of my mouth at the sight of her blood rolling down my arm and plopping on my foot.

"Put her down. I was the one who hit you."

Grandmother threw me to the unforgiving ground. Ann ran to my side. "Go with Granddaddy."

"I want to go home, Ann. Tell Mother I will be good please."

Granddaddy took me in his arms. "I have had enough now, Lil. These chil'ren need to go home to their momma. Ann, go over to the phone box and get in touch with Hattie Mae right now. Lauren, Lauren, get your behind over here and care for Maggie. I am going to take your grandmother over to the hospital to stitch her head up. You, chil'ren, better behave while we gone. Ann, make sure you get in touch with Hattie Mae by the time we get back."

Ann finally contacted Mother, and she got on the next Greyhound bus. Grandmother got eighty-nine stitches in her head and swore she would never forgive us. We went back to her house the following summer. But when it ended, she put us all on the bus and sent us home. Ann never told her it was Richard who actually hit her with the cinderblock. After all was said and done, someone asked how in the hell that cinderblock did not kill her? We had to wait two weeks after Richard threw it to find out. When he ran out of the house, he ran all the way back to New York. He said other than the fact that the cinderblock broke in two after it hit her the first time he did not know. Though we laugh about it now, we realized (after we got home) it was wrong to try and kill her. He said the cinderblock hit her three times. First in the rear end, it broke in half, then in the middle of her back, and one half fell to the floor. Then the head, talk about God having his hands on you.

As Ann ascended in rank, she became distant to the entire family. She constantly picked arguments with Paige, and I rose to every occasion. It got to the point that her homecomings always came with a lecture about not bothering Ann and ignoring the little things, to keep down hard feeling. My question was how could we all bother her? Except Lauren of course! We did not bother each other when she was not there, nor did we argue nearly as much as when she was not there. The arguments occurred when she came home. Mother argued with us to say what she wanted to say to her. Yes, we would get yelled at or punished for stuff she wanted to do or say to Ann. She still does it today, but now I speak up. I always hated that. Do not say something to me about something someone else did. When I am caught, I own up to what I have done. (I will take you down with me, depending on the circumstances.) Mother never says what she wants or do not want to the intended person, especially Ann. She put it off on others and expects them to understand what was being said or done was really for her. What type of shit is that? Mother should just say (in my mind this is how it should go down), "Look, you ungrateful little motherfucker, I am sick and tired of all your bullshit. I sold my good pussy to get your phony ass where you are today. You better stop giving it to people to kiss because the same people you saw on your way up is the same motherfuckers you are going to see on your way back down! And we are tired of hearing about how broke you are. Even though everybody knows you are only saying that because you don't want anybody (except Lauren) to ask your trifling ass for something. GET OVER YOURSELF!" Well, okay, that is something I would say, but I would love to put those words in Mother's mouth. Damn none of us got a pony for our sixth birthday—let it go. I hate the attitude, "I didn't get such and such for my birthday when I was ten years old. Or you were not there when I was seven. Bitch, you are kicking sixty years old in the ass! I wish Paige and Ann both would let it go and walk away." You are grown-ass women. Ann has been around the world three times over, had a fabulous career, met people, and seen things most of us will only read about in books. Buy your own damn pony. Despite the fact that you can does not mean you have to rub it in other people's faces, however.

Ann always said how spoiled Roddy and I were. There were many times I wanted to say, "You must be out of your cotton-picking mind. You have the nerve to say we are spoiled. We are the ones on the front lines dealing with the aftermath of what she did to help you. Getting our asses tore up when you come home because Mother was too weak to tell you what a selfish bitch you are. And when you are not here we have to pick her drunken ass up and carry her through!

Our relationship tends to be a bit hit or miss. The same can be said about Ann and Paige for that matter. I will say they have gotten better. Depending on what day it is and time also. Each has a hair trigger and a short fuse. Paige differs from me in the fact that she does not know when to call it quits and just take her ass home. She sticks around until it blows up in her face. Maybe that is what she wants to happen. They dwell in the past. Paige just stop wearing baby hair slicked down her temples two years ago. Me, I am past that. When they vacation together, I say, "That's okay, so and so has this event, or that event, so I cannot make it." Sure enough, one of them (usually Lauren) will call me in tears and say, "This is absolutely the last time I am going on vacation with the two of them. The very next year I get the same phone call. It is always during the witching hour too. I keep telling everyone nothing good goes on after midnight. That is the time when the devil is out and about doing his best work. Think about it. Nothing is open at that time except 7-Eleven, and legs. If Big Sexy says he's thirsty, I ride with his ass to get something to drink. Hattie Mae ain't raise no fool!

It is like Paige needs Ann to validate how far she has come. Why exactly? I do not know. In my opinion, Paige feels slighted. She wants the things Ann achieved. The accolades, super career, world travel, and adulation, just the chance of achieving anything was snatched away from her because of Mother's inability to . . . There lies the inception of an intrinsic battle of what could have been and what actually is. This dichotomy created a lifetime of surreptitious backstabbing, bickering, and sibling rivalries. But if that is what defines you at the end of the day, what does that say about Paige? Who is being the selfish one now? Not appreciating what God has blessed you with. Bringing you through it, to get to it, and you still acting like you are a teenager waiting for us to get off the school bus. If there is one quality I can identify with in Ann, is she will keep it moving with the quickness! She does not care who she has to step over to get there either.

Ann and I do have our disagreements from time to time. There have been times when we have not spoken for upward of a year. I always give in and reach out to her. We will do well for a while, but something always happens to change that. I will say since she has retired from the military her ego has deflated, a bit. At the end of the day, behind closed doors, when you are all alone, when those so-called friends are gone, the money does not give you the same rush as it once did, and a superstar career has come to an end, your family will always be there. I am no longer jealous of what she had the courage to do, maybe a bit envious at times. But hell, who isn't every now and then. Ann might be sitting in her fabulous home thinking, "The grass is greener on my side of the fence," who knows? Even though she will not accept it, she will always be my superhero. It was because of her I learned that women can fly! That is why I will always reach out to you. *I love you, Rasputia*!

Lauren,

Hope in itself is derived out of an eternal spring from which you drink. When your spring runs low, you gladly sacrifice without hesitation. Remember, however, if expectation is not denied, it dictates dangerous pamper to those coddled indulgences.

Sister, some of the best times I ever had were with you, and I hope in turn you can indeed say the same. If I never visit those days again, I am content in the fact that we were queens for more than a day! Our reign, some may think inconsequential, but for us, none could do it better. Long gone are the days when we rocked the party, but I do not doubt that we still could. Older yes, wiser definitely! For wisdom is gained through experience, and let's just say if experience is needed for the job we are well qualified!

GOOD TIMES, BETTER MEMORIES, GREATEST LOVE OF ALL SISTERHOOD!

Spend It All Now, Because You Can't Take With You!

Lauren and I have the same father. I do not know if that complete mixture of DNA made us have more in common by way of partying, a good scheme, and our way of thinking. It could be because we are both Libras, who really knows? If Paige was my second mother, then Lauren was definitely one of my closest friends. We had a lot of crazy times together. I do not think it was because we are sisters. I genuinely like her as a person. She never judged me, at least not to my face.

Of all the sisters and brothers, Lauren is probably the closet to Mother. They are like two peas in a pod. Paige says Lauren is the prodigal daughter. She will be upset after reading this, but Paige has always been envious of their relationship. She wants the relationship with Mother that Lauren has, and she was not the only one either. Ann coveted that position as well. Who could blame them? Everyone wants a good relationship with their parents. Me myself I do not care. I consider myself to be a lone wolf. Well, maybe on some level I did. But I will tell you this that relationship has never been healthy for either of them. They enable one another's temptation for the forbidden fruit. Although we all have an individual relationship with Mother, each one different. Equally we provided her what she needed to survive. Lauren's was to baby her. Always coming to her aide, not to say the rest of us did not. But the rest of us would say enough is enough, whereas Lauren constantly made excuse after excuse for her. In those situations, she should have stood strong against the wind.

I tease her because she looks more and more like Mother every time I see her. All she needs is a big pair of tinted glasses and a humongous dirty blonde wig or weave. I will be damn if Hattie Mae is not twenty-five years younger, of course with five less children and only one baby daddy.

Well, actually husband. What is ironic is both Mother and Lauren married men that they did not stay with, each of their firstborn is a girl, and their second born are boys who were born less than a year after the first. How freaky is that? But after her second child, Lauren knew when to say when.

Growing up with her was different than being grown and hanging with her. We had the typical big-sister, little-sister issues. She only cared for me when she was made to do so, which, to say the least, she despised with a passion. Mother always made Lauren wash and braid my hair when Paige was MIA. I was happy when Paige or Lauren combed it. They made it look pretty. But never Ann because she is heavy-handed and has no sense of style. She would style it any ole kind of way just to be done. Mother would make Lauren re-comb my hair just as she was about to go out with her friends or on a date. Oh my goodness, I hated those times. I know she did it to mess with her. I do not think Mother knew Lauren took her frustrations out on my head. But no matter how angry she was, her work never looked like it. The middle of my head is still tender to this very day. When I go to the beauty salon and the person combs over that spot, I automatically tense up. The person always says, "Oh, you are so tender headed." I reply, "No, I am having flashbacks."

Everyone knows shit rolls downhill, fast. That bitch would dig the teeth of the comb in my scalp, and if I cried or said anything, she would yank my hair and say, "Keep still." The bass in her voice made her sound like a man. Or she would hit me in the head with the back of the comb. Remember that scene in *The Color Purple* when Celie was combing the little girl's hair after Mister slapped her? Exactly! Would you believe that is her favorite movie? Everyone calls her Celie. Well, actually Ann does, and of course she is Nettie. (No, I am not privy to a nickname. It is just for the two of them.) There is a seven-year gap between us, when I was ten she was seventeen. Suffice it to say, we were not interested in many of the same things. She was interested in boys and partying. I was interested in Scooby Doo and food. Lauren did not let any dust get under her feet. She was very popular and hung out with a fast crowd of girls. Nice girls, but fast. For those of you who need me to break it down, fast equals grown for their age. Then again some of those bitches were downright hoes. My sister included. Lauren definitely took after Mother in that regard. When we attended the school of Hattie Mae, whereas I learned lessons of survival, she learned, douche cost money; so do not give your pussy away for free! No, she was not a hooker or anything like that. And I'm not saying she was a gold digger, but she didn't date any broke n—. Don't act like you do not know the lyrics.

Lauren was always getting into some sort of trouble, and Mother was always there to check her on it. Her trouble more often than not surrounded a boy. One evening, Tack's phone rang, and it was the guidance counselor from Westbury High School.

"Hello, may I speak to the parent of Lauren."

"Hold on."

"Hattie, someone from Lauren's school is on the phone."

"Hello, this is Lauren's mother."

"I am calling to inform you that Lauren is in danger of being retained."

"What and just why is that?"

"She has missed eighty-three days of school."

"Eighty-three days of school!"

"Yes, almost one half of the school year."

"That is impossible because I see Lauren, her sister Ann, and her brother Brian get on the bus every morning. As well as returned at the end of the day. She may have a few absences due to illness, but there is no way in hell it is anyway near eighty-three days."

(Ghetto girl—with the neck snap) Oh no, you didn't think you were going to call and tell Hattie Mae something about one of her "kidz." I don't think so. 'Cause she knew what all her "kidz" would do and not do for that fact. *Not*! Half the time she did not know what the hell we were doing and Lauren took full advantage of that.

The guidance counselor responded, "Yes, Lauren got on the bus, but she would stop the driver a few blocks away and get off. At the end of the day, she would get back on the bus at one of the stops and ride home."

"Why would the bus driver allow her to get on and off the bus?"

"Although the bus driver has been reprimanded, it is not his job to tell the student what to do! Discipline begins at home."

Mother was beyond upset. Someone told her, on the sly, that she was not doing her job correctly.

"Excuse me, I discipline my children."

"Several notices were sent home, by mail, and Lauren, requesting a parent-teacher conference immediately."

Poor Lauren, I thought the more I eavesdropped on the conversation. I prayed that she would just get hit with the belt, and not with what was at hand especially *the stick*. The more I listened, however, the more I knew it was going to be biblical. For one reason, Mother was not talking in her fake white lady voice, and second, it involved school. You could get away with many things, but causing a problem in school was not one of them.

You must understand these were not the days of teachers going to jail for dating students, teachers beating up the students, or students cursing out the teachers. This was the very early eighties when teachers were supernatural beings, and their words were still law in my house anyway. If they said you did it, you did it, even if you didn't do it. What it boiled down to was, Lauren could not miss any more days no matter what, and she would have to attend summer school. Mother agreed to the guidance counselor's terms and told him he would not have any further issues from her.

That was not the end of it, however. She had to be made example of to warn off any would-be followers. It is cases like this that mimicked what Mother did to us, that made Child Protective Services, as prevalent as it is today. I was in my room, and Lauren burst through the door. Why, she came to my room, I don't know, because I was not going to help her. My guess is that was the first place she thought of to hide. She closed the door behind her and hid in the back of my closet. You know that saying the quiet before the storm, it's true. There is a moment before all hell breaks loose, in which the hairs on the back of your neck stands up, and you get goose bumps on your arm. Well, it's called the raft of Hattie Mae. For a brief instance I thought I was on the streets of Pamplona, Spain, as that bull charged through the door. Breathing steam out of her flared nostrils, she knocked over everything in her path. Myself included. She stopped, leaned in close, and looked at me, with her bloodshot eyes. The demonic voice that came out of her mouth frightened me. "Where in the hell is she?" In my confused state, I pointed at the closet.

Yes, I know, I sold her out; but one of Mother's top five isms is, "Self-preservation is key, Maggie." Why should I have gotten my ass whipped because of Lauren's stupidity? By the time I regained my senses, I saw Lauren getting gored by Mother's sharp horns. She screamed for anyone and everyone to come and help her with each blow she received. I ran out of the room, screaming that Mother was killing Lauren. By the time they got Mother off her, she was literally broken, bloody, and we needed a new broom. She lay there on my bedroom floor with her leg twisted in an unnatural position crying. I stood there feeling guilty about giving her up. But relieved in the fact that it was not me lying there next to her for not telling where she was.

After they returned from the hospital, our house was put on lockdown. Lauren had a dislocated knee and a brace on her leg. She had bruises and scratches on her arms and face. Both her lips on one side of her face were busted. She look like she had been through hell and back, but she was in school the next day. I told you Hattie Mae don't play. Her leg never healed correctly after that beat down. To this day, her kneecap will slip out of joint. I am the only person who knows how to pop it back in place. Although they did not participate in Lauren's game of musical buses, Ann and Brian got beat down too. They along with the rest of the house were put on punishment. After the raft of Hattie Mae subsided, Lauren walked a fine line or at least limped one anyway. She attended school every day and pulled up her grades.

In fact she got so good at walking on the straight narrow that one day she missed the school bus, so she walked. On her way the neighbor's pet, Boxer, got out of the fence and attacked her. She managed to get away from the dog and continued to school. Blood dripped down her arms and legs. Although it sounds cliché, as soon as she walked through the school doors, she fainted. Though she was bitten, several times she was okay. The only thing she knew was that beat down Mother gave her was far worse than any dog could ever do!

What Mother did not know was even though Lauren was attending school every day, she was jumping out of the window at night, to meet up with the flavor of the month. That flavor was never just vanilla or chocolate. It had to have as many additives as possible for her to enjoy. Chocolate with nuts, fudge, marshmallow, and whip cream. She did however make the exception one time. When she dated Clark, we were all like what the heck because he was as vanilla as they came. (No, he was not white. I am speaking metaphorically.) Clark was just as his name sounds. Dull as a bucket of rocks. Do I have to hand feed you everything? Think about it, have you ever met or heard of a thug named Clark? No. But what he did have going for him was he was a local DJ with notoriety throughout the hood. I have to admit he was good at what he did. If there was a party, his crew was most likely the DJ.

He was crazy about her, and so was his Mother for that matter. Mother liked him, but she was not crazy about him. He was too straight and narrow; you know the kind of person I am talking about. The type of person who is not satisfied with his life; therefore, he not only has aspirations of a better one, but actually works toward achieving it. He was a really nice guy too. She seemed happy with him and got in far less trouble.

Every Christmas, Mother gave me twenty-five dollars to buy gifts. Remember this was the eighties, gas was not a million dollars and buying a gallon of milk did not cost as much as the whole dang cow. Lauren and Clark took me to the Mid Island Plaza. (Yes, the infamous mall Mother and I fell down the escalator, and she left me to limp out in embarrassment alone.) Lauren ditched me on him as soon as we got there. He patiently walked with me for hours as I shopped. There was a vendor outside one of the stores. She was selling wooden plaques in the shape of a teapot, with big hand-painted flowers. I knew that was the gift for Mother, but I did not have enough money. It was thirteen dollars. I will never forget it. But I do forget how much I had, sorry. It does not matter, because you know how the story ends. I told you he was just nice like that.

Lauren was a different person with him; her wild ways all but disappeared, his aspirations seemingly rubbed off on her. After she graduated from high school, she enrolled in community college and found a job at a senior citizen nursing home as a nurse's aide. She wanted to be a nurse. We were all taken by surprise with that one. It was not because she was stupid.

Until you consider the most important dynamic in her plight, for upward mobility, you will not understand her difficulty achieving it. She has a weak constitution. That bitch will throw up if you throw up. Certain smells, especially blood, even bugs will make her hurl her cookies. I should know because to pay her back for many of the things she did to me, I would make her throw up just for general purposes. Yes, I know I am a stinker. I told you I am weird, and I embrace it.

Her nursing career went nowhere fast. She did complete the two-year program however. Other than the fact that she came home from work sicker than her patients, she would have made a great nurse. On the other hand, they don't just hire you for your good bedside manner. You actually have to do something medically related. I am not sure, but you probably have to assist doctors, administer medication, and clean a bedpan or two. I am sure however, you cannot pass out at the sight of blood, guts, or shit. Suppose a gunshot victim come through the doors with half of his brains lying on the pillow next to him and you hit the floor. Or a heart attack victim come in and they crack open his chest and you hit the floor. Or a homeless lady come in with lice, stinking to the high heavens, puking her guts out because the sandwich of the day from *Garbage Can De Jour* gave her food poisoning and your ass hit the floor. Do you see where I am going with this? That career choice was doomed from the start. Needless to say, it did not last long and neither did Clark.

Lauren found her niche as an office worker, but such a monotonous job and a squeaky-clean boyfriend was not a good mix. Old habits can die hard and will find a way to rear their ugly head, especially when you are bored out of your mind. True to form, being her mother's protégé, her drug of choice was a hot-blooded man, drama preferred. Bad boys only need to apply.

Excitement walked through the door in the reincarnated form of Randy Baker. His younger brother, Jake, was just her type. How happy must his mother have been to see yet another one of Hattie Mae's daughters sauntering through her kitchen door? What was the dinner conversation like the night he told her who he was dating? Imagine sitting at that table eating and discussing the day's events. To be a fly on the wall that night, in my mind it went something like this:

"How was your day, dear? I made your favorite meal, pot roast, mashed potatoes, peas and carrots, and for dessert peach cobbler."

"Oh, it was great. I got an A in algebra and asked Lauren Stephens to be my girlfriend."

"You did what? Are you out of your fucking mind? Just when I got rid of the other one, you go and bring another one of them in here. What is it about those girls anyway that you and your brother can't stay away from?"

"They got good pussy. Pass the peas and carrots please."

Well, I imagine it happening like that anyway, even if you cannot see my vision. Actually from what I understand, Glenda loved Lauren. Of course Mother welcomed Jake with open arms. Especially after the way he made his grand entrance. It was a Saturday morning. Some things you just never forget. I was still in my body cast from breaking my leg. My friend Althea stayed over as she did most weekends. It was about 5:30 maybe 6:00 a.m., and we were awoken to a woman screaming bloody murder. We waited a moment and heard it again, but this time it sound like she was on the move. Not being mobile, I sent Althea to be my eyes and ears.

She ran back in the room with Mother close behind her. "Althea, get your ass back in the bed and do not come out of this room again." As she left, she closed the door behind her so we could not hear. Underestimating Althea's skills, she did not see her creep out behind her. By the time she was noticed, she had already got the jest of the story.

Althea said, "Lauren cheated on Clark with someone named Jake. She snuck out the window last night to be with him. He just dropped her off." Her arms flared wildly as she spoke much too fast. "Clark suspected something and has been sitting outside your house with his friend all night." She paused and took a deep breath. "When Lauren got out of Jake's car, Clark confronted them. Jake chased Clark into the house. That was Clark screaming for help." She doubled over in laughter.

"Oh no, the girl we thought was screaming was actually him."

She whispered, "Jake kicked his ass."

That day was officially the end of "Laurk" and was the beginning of "Lake." Whoever created making two names into one should be punched in the face. "Brangelina," "Benniffer," all of it is stupid.

Lauren and Jake were inseparable. You could not tell where she began and he ended and vice versa. I am not going to say I liked him at that time because he was not Clark. Hell, he wasn't even Randy. Whereas Clark was easygoing and sweet and Randy had a criminal mentality but he was genuinely a good person, Jake however always seemed to be plotting something. He tried to befriend me, but I did not warm up to him and neither did Roddy. It was something about him. But damn if Mother was not his biggest fan. Within a year, Lauren was pregnant, and he enlisted in the Air Force.

Mother was livid. She kept saying, "I am going to be the one to end up taking care of that baby. The reason he enlisted was to get out of his responsibility." Everything that she experienced with her ex's was put on Lauren.

I came home from school one day, and Mother was nonstop at her. Paige had moved to Alabama some months previously. So Lauren had to defend herself. She was crying and not feeling well. Never in a million years could we have imagined what would happen next. She was most definitely at her breaking point to yell at Mother.

"I am married and have been for several months."

Mother stood in disbelief. The expression on her face was as if she was thinking what the word married meant. The only thing I was thinking was damn she is going to break her other leg! Lauren went to her room and came back with all the proof she needed to shut Mother's mouth, if only for a moment. She gave her an Air Force Military insurance ID card with her picture and name on it. Lauren Sheldon was written in stone.

They decided to tell everyone after he completed basic training. Except now she told us. Telling her family first and going against his wishes started a precedent of positioning one family over the other. It was exactly the way Mother wanted it. There was just too much history between the two families. Randy and Paige and now Lauren and Jake. I know Glenda said thank goodness she has no more sons to sacrifice on Hattie Mae's alter of fire. However, there are two sisters, but they are older than my brothers. Actually, now that I think about it, there is that crazy cousin, who was Randy's partner in crime.

Glenda was a lady in every sense of the word. She was at least six feet tall, statuesque, and very nice looking. Not a cougar but she was one of those older women who really kept up on her looks, clothes, hair, cars, and house. What I liked about her was though feministic, she did not depend on anyone. She had a great job at the Grumman Aircraft Engineering Corporation, which in the past produced military and civilian aircrafts. Grumman was one of two jobs that the majority of Westbury people worked. It was the job a lot of Westbury residents aspired to have. Roosevelt Raceway was the other.

Both Grumman and Roosevelt Raceway afforded minority families the opportunity to live like their counterparts. Glenda worked at Grumman for almost twenty years. After her divorce, she moved her family to an affluent suburb. She loved to party and would invite friends and family to her home for pool parties and barbeques. The only other home I saw as nice as hers in a minority area was my father's in the Hamptons. Lauren would take me and a friend to her parties, and we would spend the day luxuriating at her expense. I do not know why, but I always had the feeling Glenda did not care for me.

Maybe she thought I was looking at her with judgmental eyes. I wasn't though; actually, there was something about her I liked. I sensed that she too had a dark side no one knew about. Yet those eyes looked at me like, "Get away, you weird little girl, and stop eating up all my food." Or maybe she suspected the same about me. Her mother, Jake's grandmother, was a different story. She was as sweet as pie, with ice cream and a cherry on the top. Everyone called her Big Mama, and yes she looked just like the name sounds. She was the cook at the Head Start program I attended and was heavy-set with big breast. Every time she hugged me, she'd smothered my face in her bosom. It felt safe there, and she always smelled like Sunday dinner, complete with her famous peach cobbler for dessert. You know I love food and so did she. Believe it or not, as a child I was a big cry baby. The teachers would tire of me crying and send me down to the office. Big Mama would come get me and take me to the kitchen where she would hug and kiss me until I would stop crying. I can vaguely remember sitting in her lap as she stroked my hair. Years later, I would visit her at her senior living apartment, and she would cook something for us to eat. And I do not mean ramen noodles. She could cook, no recipe book required. Leave your measuring cup and spoons at home. Her method of a little of this, and a pinch of that had you licking the skin off your fingers. I would usually bring us ice cream for dessert. We talked about nothing in particular. It was nice and quiet at her place. I really miss those times with her.

That said, a baby girl was delivered, and Jake moved them to Missouri where he was stationed. Not long after they left, Lauren returned home. That was not the first time she made a quick exodus, and it definitely was not her last. The first time she left she was eight months pregnant. The night before her departure, she came to my room and got in bed with me. Although it was dark, I knew she was crying. Her big belly shook the whole bed. She said she was scared to leave me behind and was sorry she could not take me with her. I was thirteen years old and basically about to be on my own. But for her sake, I put on a brave face and said, "You know me. I will be fine." As we continued to talk, she took my hand and put it on her balloon belly. The baby was kicking, and I knew that we would be close. She made it home just in time for Quan to be born.

The second time she came back, I did not care why, because that baby girl was the joy of my life, all our lives. She saved me from myself. I always joke with her and tell her she is really my daughter, and I just wanted her back. I gave birth to her through Lauren's vagina, ill I know. But it makes her laugh. She was with me more than she was with Lauren. With Jake still in Missouri, Lauren became very depressed. She never discussed what was wrong with her. I thought it was because his visits home were not long enough. Ten months later, a baby boy was born. Jake Junior became Mother's new toy. She stopped drinking and was just happy and finally stable. You would have thought she had given birth to him. That little boy did something none of the seven of us could do; she became this whole new person. With Quan with me and lil Jake with Mother, Lauren had it made, until.

Jake was discharged from the Air Force. Why, I do not know; if I did, you know I would tell you. When he returned, they lived upstairs in our house. She refused to leave Mother. They argued all the time. Our mother only intervened when the shouting became too loud in front of the children or they fought. I honestly believe that if they had moved on their own, they would have had a better chance. Getting away from both their families might have given them a better chance instead of fighting each other. I am not one to lecture because who the hell am I to cast the first stone. But when they had problems, we all had problems, because there were too many people in both their ears. Myself included! Now as a married old woman who lives in a shoe and has two kids and her mother-in-law living with us, and don't know what to do, I would like to apologize to them. Though I know I was not a major reason they parted ways, I am truly sorry for any role I played in driving a wedge between them. It is difficult enough to be married; but being young, married, with two children, and living with your wife's entire dysfunctional family cannot make it any easier. I was just looking out for my sister.

I physically attacked Jake more than once. Mind you, he is approximately six feet two, two hundred—plus pounds. I am approximately five foot five, and at that time weighed one hundred twenty pounds wet if that. I know I did not do much damage, but I did get some licks in for her. I'd jump on his back and start punching. He'd fling me on the floor and call Mother. I didn't care about the punishment. In my mind, Lauren wanted to, but was too afraid of what Mother would say. Well, you know what I say: bust him in his head now and worry about Mother later!

I can remember one such time. Mother and Tack were out; Roddy was in his room, and I was in mine. Lauren had not long come home from work. All of a sudden, you hear this loud boom noise, like something fell on the floor. Screams and curses soon followed. So I went to the bottom of the stairway and looked up and saw Roddy standing in the hallway. He mouthed they were arguing. The children were crying, so I ran up the stairs and bammed on the door. Roddy pulled me in his room. "You better not get involved."

"Why aren't you? You hear the kids in there."

"Mother said to mind our business. You better go back downstairs because you know Jake is going to tell on you."

Why he wasted his breath is something you will have to ask him. I snatched away from his grasp and knocked on the door again.

"If you do not open the door, I will call the police." I ran down the stairs and picked up the handset.

"Hello 911. What is your emergency?"

"Yes, can you please send someone to my home? I think my brother-in-law killed my sister."

"Why would you think such a thing?"

"They were arguing, and their two children were crying."

"So children are on the premises. Are they still fighting?"

"It's quiet now, but I cannot get in the room."

"A car is in route. Stay on the phone until it arrives. Is anyone else in the home?"

"Just my punk-ass brother. He is in his room. He said he is not getting involved."

"Wait for the officers outside."

"Okay."

The police came and spoke with both of them, with her busted lip and his scratched-up face. After the police had gone, Jake must have gotten me confused with her because he jumped up in my face. Well, he did not jump in my face because he towered over me.

"What is your problem?" His finger poked my nose with every word he spoke.

My philosophy is the bigger they are, the harder they fall. "You don't scare me. I will cut your ass down to size." If you have not realized this yet, I have a potty mouth, which was one of the main things I got in trouble for when I was young.

"You are not going to keep jumping on me. I will knock your little dumb ass out in here."

The next thing I knew I leaped on his ass and began fighting like my life depended on it. He was just trying to get me off him. I was already going to catch a beat down from Mother, so hey. It took Lauren, Roddy, and him to subdue me. Later that night when Mother returned home, I got cursed out and put on punishment for one interfering in their marriage, two calling the police, and three attacking Jake. I didn't see daylight for a month of Sundays. For those of you who do not understand what that means, it's a really long time. After that we came to a mutual understanding. Don't put your hands on my sister and I will not put my hands on you. It didn't matter because she ended up leaving him and moving to North Carolina with Ann.

It wasn't three months after she left New York that Mother came to me and said, "I am leaving Tack and moving to North Carolina. You need to decide what you are going to do. I know you don't want to leave James, but I am out."

I knew what it was and wasn't upset. Actually I did not think she would last that long with Lauren and the kids gone. Things did not work out for me after Mother left, so I relocated too. Mother purchased a beautiful home with an in-ground pool. Lauren and her children did not move with us though; she stayed with Ann. They were at Mother's far more than they were at Ann's. Lauren became a different person. Our relationship changed in the process. We were more friends than big sister, little sister.

This is where the fun began. After I turned twenty-one, there wasn't too much anyone could tell me. But I did listen within reason to Paige and Lauren. Paige, not being in North Carolina in the beginning, left it up to Lauren to keep me in check. Lauren always had a way of bringing the worse out of me—from stealing Pampers and milk so we could keep Jake's money to daring me to drink Tack's good scotch that was hidden in the back of his closet. After Richard's death and Roddy went to jail (the first time), I was on a serious downward spiral. Spinning out of control, Lauren tried to keep me close. She was always there to push the stop button. I think she felt guilty about the time she turned her head for one second.

One night she stole Tack's car and was going to her friend's house. I caught her as she was going out the door and told her if she did not take me with her I was going to tell. We picked up a few other people along the way, and the party began. I had a drink or two. We formed a circle (like spin the bottle); someone lit a joint and sent it around clockwise. Then someone else lit another joint and sent it around counterclockwise. The one that I was smoking was counterclockwise and had a funny taste to it. Almost sweet but I knew candy wasn't in it. But that need to belong kept me puffing. Lauren emerged from wherever she was and pulled me out of the circle. She must have slapped me because although I couldn't feel it, I do remember my face flinging from side to side.

"Cindy, what did ya'll give my sister?"

"We smoked some weed."

"What was in it?"

"One was just weed, and the other had powder in it."

"Cocaine, you gave her cocaine! What the fuck, Cindy."

"She wanted to do it."

"She knew it was cocaine?"

"Well, we didn't say it, but everyone knows the counterclockwise joint has something in it."

"She's thirteen. How would she know that? I am so fucked."

The next thing I remember we were in the car sitting in the drive-through line at McDonald's. As we pulled away from the window, her friend shoved French fries in my mouth. Lauren slammed on the brakes, and I flew forward and hit the back of the front driver seat. Lauren yelled, "Roddy, what are you doing?"

"Mother sent me to look for ya'll. She said you better bring Tack's car home now." He walked over to the car. "Maggie, you want to ride home with me?" He had not long purchased this big blue monster pickup truck, and he had it pimped out with lights and duel exhaust. "Mag, Mag? Lauren, what's wrong with her? She looks weird."

"I don't know. You know she's always playing some stupid game."

"Maggie, quit playing. No, Lauren, something's not right. Her lips moving, but she's not saying anything." In my mind I was holding a whole conversation with them. "I am calling Mother right now."

"No, wait, okay, it's not my fault, but she got hold of a joint with coke in it."

"Are you crazy?" He pulled me out of the car and put me in his truck. "She smells like she's been drinking too." He squealed off, and the next thing I remember was waking up the next day and not seeing daylight for another month of Sundays.

North Carolina turned out to be the best thing for all of us. Not being told to get out or moving around town every other week was refreshing. After the novelty wore off, we needed an outlet. Leave it to Lauren to find every party hole in town. We tore the clubs up. It got to the point where the party wouldn't start until we got there. She was probably the most stable of the club kids. Although she was the one who usually got the party started, she made sure everyone made it home safely, except this one particular Thursday night. She had been driving over ten hours after spending a week in New York.

"Are you trying to go to LaRocca tonight?"

"No, I am too tired."

"Come on. We have this rental van for one more night and can pick everybody up. I don't feel like going home." Her solemn expression said it all. Things did not go well for her and Jake in New York.

"All right, so how are we going to do this?"

"I will drop you and Mother off at home, then I will go home and give the kids a bath. I will take a hoe bath. Then I will bring them back to Mother's and pick you up. While I'm gone call everyone to find out who wants to come. Tell them we will pick them up on the way."

"Did you ask Mother to babysit?"

"Nope, and I am not going to because I do not want to hear her mouth that I must be tired from driving. So when you see the kids come in the house, just come out."

"What?"

"They just gonna go get in the bed with her anyway. She'll think I'm on the couch. We will be back long before she figures it out."

"All right, it's on you."

About ten of us walked through the club doors and the crowd cheers. No lie. We knew the majority of the crowd there, and instantly some of us hit the dance floor. Lauren and a few others hit the bar, and she drank a beer. This was unusual for her; she never drank when we were out. I kept dancing, and by the next song I saw her drinking a second beer. Then she puked right there. I ran to her. "Are you okay?"

"I need some air."

"Come on. I'll go with you."

"No," she snapped. "I don't want you coming with me. Go back and dance. I am all right."

"Benny, can you go outside with Lauren?"

"Sure."

Moments later, he ran back in and said she vomited again and was passed out in the back of the van. I drove everyone home and tried my best to get her in the house without waking Mother. As soon as she saw the headlights in the driveway, she flung open the front door. After we put Lauren to bed, Mother informed me that things between her and Jake were worse than I knew. He begged her to return to New York so they could be together. Lauren refused to leave Mother. They decided to remain separated and move on with their lives. Whatever that means?

That might have been the end of their relationship, but it caused our partying to go in overdrive. Lauren was always that fun sister, always pushing me beyond my limits. Many of my firsts are attributed to her. My first drink of alcohol; I could never turn down a dare. Even my first love (What's up, Big Sexy), when Mother went in one direction, Lauren would drop me off at his house and go in her direction. Those were the sweetest days. Going over James's house for an afternoon tryst, taking baths together, and then him making us lunch. That's why I am a stay-at-home mom. I will be damn if I go out the front door and someone is sneaking in the back. Our son is a little devil, and he is a junior in every sense of the word. He is a combination of his father and my brothers Brian and Roddy. I'm watching the doors and windows!

I was in my first shootout because Lauren just had to introduce our friend Valerie to this guy. Yes, this is the night before we were to attend Ann's big award ceremony and parade. What Lauren didn't tell Valerie was that this club had one way in and one way out and was in the heart of the hood. You know the kind of place—when you walk in, your feet sticks to the floor, and you look at the glass before you take your first sip. (By the third drink, you don't care anymore and just keep drinking.) What you must understand about Valerie is she's afraid of her own shadow and would never have gone there.

Of course it was as if we had taken cliché 101 from the Hood Club handbook directly from the pages, an altercation between these two guys brokeout and they fought. I was ready to go when it first began. But since the guy who started it was escorted out, we kept on partying. The next thing I know I hear pop, pop, pop! I kept dancing until I saw Lauren crawling on the floor toward me waving for me to get down. Not knowing what she was signing, I stood there.

When she reached me, she tugged at my skirt and said, "Get down, bitch. Don't you see they shootin' up in here?"

"Is that what that was? I thought that was part of the song! I'm not getting on the floor. This is a new outfit."

Pop, pop, pop, pop, pop! "Get your dumb ass on the floor and cover your head."

"Uh no, this outfit is new."

Even though the bullets were flying overhead, I knew those stains were not going to come out of what I was wearing. They weren't ordinary suburban stains that Mother could scrub out with some Tide. *These were hood stains!* I have to admit though I got excited after I was in the car and on my way home. During the shootout, I was bargaining, "Jesus, if you let me survive this, I will never . . ." You know the drill!

Although she was always getting me into something, she was always there when I needed her to get me out of something just the same. We were at LaRocca one Saturday night. This new guy asked me to dance. So I said yes; it was just a dance, right? Wrong! We danced a few songs, and I introduced him to everyone. Then he danced with someone else. So I sat down. When he came back to the table, he bought me a drink. I accepted not thinking anything of it. Literally within seconds, the room began seesawing, and I was moving but do not remember walking. I thought I was in a Spike Lee movie, you know when he does that floating special effects thing with the camera. I could not get enough air. My new friend rushed over to me. What I said to him I do not remember, but I do remember him constantly smiling in my face as he walked me toward the door. Before we exited, Lauren stopped him from taking me outside. I was on fire and sweating. She asked what did he give me, and he would only admit to giving me a drink. I vomited foam and dropped to my knees. Lauren and some friends carried me out and took me home. It seem like every five minutes we had to stop for me to puke more foam. The next day I had the hangover from hell. I never found out what he spiked my drink with. His mistake was he had told one of our friends where he lived. Although we waited about a week, Lauren and I went to his house and flattened all four of his tires!

Lauren lives a semi-quiet life. She is the grandmother of seven beautiful children, how times changes. Every time I hear one of them calling "Me-Ma" I laugh. What the heck is a Me-Ma? It sounds like he-ha. If she likes it, I love it, and I know she does. She does the whole granny thing quite well. That is until it is "Me-Ma" time, and all their asses have to go home. She is after all only forty-nine. Bernie Mack was right; these days Mama is twenty-nine, Grandma is forty-nine, and Big Mama is sixty-nine—and they all partying at the same club.

Hey, SISTER POWER!

His Divine Plan

I had often asked myself why Mother had so many damn kids, especially if she was not financially, mentally, but above all, emotionally prepared to take care of them. That question followed me throughout the better part of my life, causing me to not want children, as well as dominate and push away the man who ultimately became my soul mate. This fear of loving and being loved was always there like a stalker in the night, quietly lurking in the shadow. Present like an old lover whom you greet cordially, but ask yourself, "Why in the hell . . . ?"

But who am I to judge? No one knows what God's divine plan is for any of us. Maybe that was her path to follow, having us. Her cross to bear, seven of them. We all have them. Sometimes they are not seen out right, and sometimes they are smack-dab in your face. Whatever the reason, she chose to have all of us, and I thank her, because I am here. Even though constantly reminded that I was not supposed to be, because if abortion was legal . . . , or she should have flushed my ass down the toilet when she had the chance! *I didn't forget*, though I have forgiven.

She did the best she knew how to raise us and keep us together. She could not be what I or the rest of my siblings wanted her to be, and I can now accept that. I pray they can do the same. Could she have done better by us? Hell yeah, but we survived. Some of us, even stronger, though some forever weakened. We can all do better in one shape or form, can't we? Besides, if nothing else, she gave me six of the craziest, funniest brothers and sisters who love me to death with their trifling asses. I would not trade any one of them for nothing in the world. *I wish I could say the same for them, because for the right price, one just never knows.* One thing, of many, I've learned from them is that you can only control your own actions.

Yeah, I know you're saying, "Dang, first she tugged at our heartstrings by putting them down for her shortcomings." No, I'm not; I'm not blaming anyone for anything, just telling the damn truth as it happened. Anybody out there reading this continued journey of mine, who comes from a large family, knows exactly the drama I'm talking about. I just got the courage to put our dirty laundry out there in the street for the whole world to read. Well, not really so much courage, I just don't care what anyone thinks anymore! It has held me back far too long. I'm tired of fixing stuff. Or making it appear fixed, which by the way is even harder. Now don't take it the wrong way. It is what it is, that's all, and I have finally accepted it. This is not one of those stories ending with happily ever after. If that's what you're into, good for you, but this is not it. So close the book now, before you get pulled in any deeper into this melodrama. It's not told on a superficial level. Instead it peels away layers of predisposition, ultimately exposing where the core of character is formed and the seed of productivity is planted. The place where if nurtured correctly creates a complex dynamic in which we become all we can become. If neglected, well, just keep reading!

Brian,

Brother, we share the same childhood memories and also dreams of growing up and becoming who we would become. Together we weathered the storm, wondering in which direction the wind would blow. I'd ask a penny for your thoughts, as we tossed coins in the wishing well of life. We played that's my car and four corners. I am who I am because you are who you are. I want you to know how much I enjoy having you as my big brother.

Thinking of you brings forth some of the warmest and funniest memories. Without you, there would have been no laughter in the house. Each time you entered the door, you brought in the sunshine. The light ricocheted off your beautiful smile, illuminating the darkness. It takes special qualities to make a person like you, which some may not appreciate. Albeit I do! Even if you were not my brother, I would say the same. I am proud to have you as my brother because you are a good person as many people know. You go out of your way to help others even to the detriment of yourself. Your good deeds have not gone unnoticed. Know that I will always be there for you. Don't ever doubt that.

Tears of a Clown

Brian is and has always been a very proud man. He will not ask you to spit on him if he was running down the street on fire with gasoline boxers on. I know I will laugh through most of this. My brother is literally the brother everyone dreams of having. When we were younger, the job of babysitting Roddy and me sometimes fell on him. Every time it did, the three of us ended up in some sort of trouble when Mother returned. Brian would come up with the craziest stuff for us to do. One Christmas, Mother went out to finish her shopping. She told us that Santa was not coming to our house because we had been naughty. Roddy and I cried while Brian sat looking at us smirking. I asked him why he was not sad.

"I'll tell you after Mother leaves." We watched as she drove away with Lauren and Ann.

Brian said, "Follow me."

"You know we are not supposed to be in Lauren and Ann's room."

"Maggie, do you want to see the surprise or not? Then sit on the floor and be quiet."

He opened their closet. It was filled with presents, big ones, little ones, long ones, and short ones. He took them out one by one and carefully opened them and showed us what we had for Christmas.

When Mother returned, we were sitting in the living room. Roddy had this big dumb smile, and she asked, "Did you behave because Santa might change his mind?"

I replied, "Who cares about Santa, somebody already left a closet full of toys for us upstairs." Brian jumped to his feet and ran to his favorite hiding place, leaving me and Roddy hanging.

The best thing he ever came up with was tobogganing down the stairs, on a comforter. Brian would take his comforter and tie a knot at one end. Roddy would sit in front, me in the middle, and Brian in back. We would slide down and run back up the stairs and slide back down a thousand times. By the end of the day, our butts were sore as hell. I do not know where he came up with all the crazy things he came up with. But Roddy and I were grateful to say the least. The craziest thing he came up with would have to be the human catapult. He shared a room with Roddy and Richard. His bed was across from Roddy's. Brian would lie on his bed, on his back with his feet up in the air. As I lie across his feet, Roddy gave him coordinates of where I should land. Adjustments were made in accordance. He would bend his legs, and then he would do this kicked/push/spring action leg move as hard as he could. In theory, it was a good plan. However, either the coordinates were off or Brian's kick/push/spring action leg move was more powerful than he thought, because I went through the wall.

Another of his hair brain ideas was when he convinced Roddy that he would be braver than Evel Knievel himself if he jumped down the staircase from the second floor of our home—all thirteen steps. Roddy tied a towel around his neck and stood there for a moment. I could see that his brain was telling him not to do it, but his foolish pride won out over common sense. Always wanting to outdo, be tougher than, and outsmart Brian told him "You can win, Roddy!" He not only jumped, but also missed every step. In that instance, time slowed just enough, so that as I watched him flying through the air, he actually looked like a black nerdy Evel Knievel. But then he crashed into our two-inch-thick solid wood door and fell to the floor. When he stood, his legs wobbled; his glasses were broken in half, and his lips were busted. Before he collapsed, he smiled and said, "I did it, Brian. I am braver than Evel Knievel." Brian once again left us hanging and ran to his hiding spot. We had some really good times together, doing time on Holly Lane.

Somehow Brian always knew when I was about to snap and would say, "Hey, Mag, I just rolled a fatty. I'll light the grill, and you get the food."

Now that I think about it though, he was probably the one about to snap, and that was his way of coping. I must say this: in his defense, people might ask how he could condone me smoking marijuana at such a young age. By that point, he knew what I was doing, when I was doing it, and there was nothing he could do about it. As long as I remained a virgin, I could get as messed up as I wanted to. I could be an alcoholic pothead, but not a hoe.

"Just don't leave the yard!" Brian hated fast girls. He, like Roddy, always warned me of the dangers of crumbled cookies. "Nobody wants the crumbs, Maggie, or why buy the cow if the milk is sour." But they in turn were two of the biggest whores in town, actually several of them.

After we smoked the fatty and ate, he would complain about his love life. Then he had the nerve to say, "I'll be back." Do you know how many times he blew my high, sitting there listening to him go on about what's her name? To this day he is still complaining about her crazy ass! After thirty years, kill that bitch, or leave her, or something. I am just saying. I know you are going to catch all kinds of hell for that one. I can hear her now. (You all must imagine her voice sounds like a record playing too damn fast, yes it is annoying, especially when she is angry. Add in her Jamaican accent and you can't understand a word she is saying.) "Brian, why is your sister making fun of me? Brian, Brian, do you hear me talking to you, Brian? Why is she calling me, what's her name? Brian, who doesn't she want to know my name, Brian? Who you sleeping with now, Brian? I am going to wash your dick with bleach, Brian." Everything with her is a threat or question, never an answer. *Shut the fuck up!* I do not know how he does it! But he loves her, and I love him. So I sit back and bite my tongue. Thank goodness I do not drink anymore. (But dang, you need to realize your worth, man. Quick! I told you what to do to her ass a long time ago. No, not that, the other thing. I am not that crazy; well, there was that one time . . . Shh, that is just between you and me. They do not need to know everything.)

Her family was well known in our small town. By New Cassel standards, they were well-to-do. Or at least they thought they were. She walked around with her nose in the air and had an attitude to match. Every time something did not go her way, she would send her sisters to our house to beat up Brian. I failed to mention one of her sisters was shaped like a linebacker. Her pastime however was fighting instead of trying to make touchdowns. I could not stand to see them coming. Mother put up with her and her family the best she knew how. There was one rule she had that every time Brian broke it, she *fucked his ass up—with the big stick!* (It was not what you think. Even though she was a virgin when they started dating, she did not remain that way.) At that time, her mother loved Brian and loved to cook for him. I do not know how the rumor started, or if it was even a rumor at all. We all know that facts can be stranger than fiction. It could be fact or fiction if Mother got wind of it that is all she needed. It was said (by our next-door neighbor) that the mother was a root doctor, or at the very least practiced voodoo. It was said that she put a root in the food she cooked Brian, and that is why he could not rid himself (and us for that matter) of that girl. Small towns have a way of hyping things up. The rumor took on a life of its own. It was said that the mother held some sort of a voodoo ceremony before the daughter was deflowered. The mother took the virgin menstruation blood and cooked in curry goat and fed it to Brian.

Mother was extremely persnickety about what came in or went out of her kitchen. The kitchen was her domain, and she ruled it with an iron fist. For the reason that just about everything she did was done from the kitchen. So much so she had several different sets of Tupperware to regulate and organize: one set for the refrigerator food she prepared; a set for people to take home food she prepared, but she did not want the container back; and another set for dry goods. You could not put anything in the refrigerator without asking her first. She had to make sure who made it, how it was made, and what was in it. Whenever Brian brought food from his girlfriend's house, Mother freaked out! So he would sneak it in the refrigerator. But the girlfriend's mother's Tupperware was totally different and stood out like a sore thumb.

One afternoon, I came home from school; when I walked in the house, I was hit in the head with a flying container of jerk chicken. Mother ushered me to the shower with all my clothes on because she believed that the root meant for Brian would get on me.

She scrubbed me like she was trying to scrub the black off and damn near drown me in the process. I thought I was getting baptized. I, however, was not the one who received the worst of it. After she threw out everything in the refrigerator and sanitized it with bleach, because in her mind everything was contaminated, she went to his room. To this day, I still believe I saw smoke coming from under the door and not from a fatty he just rolled either. Her root theory may have had some merit to it because there was something about that food that kept him trying to sneak it in.

I respect him for staying with his girlfriend though. No matter what, Brian sticks by people—some of Mother's better qualities he inherited. Brian's devoid relationship with Mother is how he would deal with all of his relationships. Not quite the womanizer he thought he was was derived out of fear to love one woman. Watching how she dealt with her relationships warped his way of dealing with his own feelings about them. He found the same woman every time: loud, argumentative, and domineering, which is surprising because he is such a good guy.

That is why everyone loves him so much, and why he had so many friends. His loyalty is to a fault and even got him thrown in jail for attempted murder. He was in eleventh grade at Westbury High School and went on a double date with his best friend, Ponz. Stupid name, but one of the coolest guys you ever want to meet. He later became one of my closest friends. I guess you could say the name was the opposite of the Fonz from *Happy Days. Not resembling the Fonz*, he wore Coke bottle glasses that I swear was so thick, he could not only see you coming a mile away, but also read your mind and tell you what you were thinking as you approached him. He had the most beautiful set of teeth. They looked like Chiclets gum and were just that white. I constantly asked him how he got his teeth so white. Especially with all the beer they drank. Brian and Ponz were always together; they were frick and frack. They were always getting into some kind of mischief. This was just one of their many, many, many crazy escapades.

They decided to take their dates to the carnival at the Nassau Coliseum. Why I cannot tell you, because in the early eighties, blacks did not patronize that carnival. If they did, it was more than four people and during daytime. Primarily because the Levittown and Hicksville residents did not want anything black near them. For years, they tried to block the New Cassel residents from using Cantiague Park. That carnival, though centrally located, was off-limits. If there is one thing you can say about small-town ideologies, they tend to be consistent across the board.

Ponz and his date entered one of the tents, but did not come out. Brian entered looking for him, and that is where the dichotomy of this story comes in play. I was sitting in the kitchen when a bam, bam, bam came on the door. Mother, who was in the back *resting*, left Roddy in charge. He opened the door and, to my surprise, stood two of the biggest white police officers I have ever seen. One of them entered uninvited and asked to speak to a parent. Roddy got Mother, who was on the last leg of sleeping one off.

She entered the kitchen and said in her caviler tone, "Good evening, Officer. How may I help you?" Though she put on a wig, her natural hair was sticking from underneath. In my head I am thinking, why is she talking like that? And what is up with her wig?

"Are you Brian's mother?"

"Yes, I am. May I ask what this is about?"

"Well, I am here to inform you—"

"Oh God, he's dead?"

Through the screen door, the other officer said, "No, but he will be if we find him first." An eerie silence fell on the room.

"Excuse me?"

"Your son has what has to be the entire Nassau County Police Department looking for him."

"For what?"

"Attempted murder."

Her hands dropped to her side as she looked at Roddy and me. We were as perplexed as she was. "Are you sure you have the right Brian? My Brian is—"

"If I did not have the right Brian, do you really think I would be wasting my time on this part of town? Now if he is here, you need to tell him to come willingly because if we find him first, I cannot guarantee it will end well."

"Sir, he's not here. You can check—" Before she got all the words out of her mouth, he motioned something at the door, and a swarm of police officers entered. I was scared as hell. I grabbed Roddy and held on to him for dear life. "Can someone please tell me what happened, because what you are accusing him of is not in his nature?"

"Not in his nature, it's in all of you people's nature. He purposely mowed down seven attendants at the carnival with his car. The only reason he was not able to run over more people was he lost control of the vehicle and flipped it."

"Oh my goodness, is he okay?"

"Ma'am, do you honestly think we give a fuck if he is okay, or not? (At least he called her ma'am.) If you hear from him, you need to get him to turn himself in." When they left, Mother was sober as a judge. If nothing else, she knew two things: one, Brian would never do what he was being accused of. And two, he would try to make his way home to her. Working as a maid for rich Jewish families had some perks, other than stealing their delicious red and golden apples for me. One of her employers gave her the name of a lawyer. The lawyer told her to go out and search for him, and he would meet them at the police station. We searched high and low. Then Mother had a revelation. "We are going over to that carnival."

The first thing we saw was his car. It was upside down and flattened like a pancake. I felt sad for him. He loved that car. Every spare moment he had he spent restoring it with the money he earned from cleaning the RKO movie theater. He would take me with him sometimes. I would sit and watch a movie as he cleaned the empty theater next to it. "Don't leave the theater. If someone comes in and bothers you, yell for me, Maggie, okay?" Seeing his car like that frightened me. Was he in there flattened too? My mind race from one bad thought to the next. I thought I would never see him again.

Mother saw Brian in the back of a squad car. He was unrecognizable. The officers kept their word and beat him to a pulp. His eyes were swollen nearly shut, his lips were busted, and blood dripped from his nose. He complained of trouble breathing and coughed up sprinkles of blood. Mother was threatened of receiving the same as she approached him. She dialed the lawyer and informed him of the situation. Moments later, she was told to follow them to Nassau County Medical Center.

There he had to be taken out of the car by orderlies because he passed out. The doctors demanded the handcuffs to be removed because they sliced into his skin. The X-rays of his chest revealed internal bruising. This could have been diagnosed by anyone looking at him. The officers left actual shoe print on his chest and back. Each blow imprinted red, blue, and purple hues on his beautiful black skin. He was admitted to the hospital and had an officer outside his room, and he was shackled to the bed until he recovered and was taken into custody.

As the facts emerged, truth prevailed. After Brian entered the tent, he found Ponz pinned to the ground and being beaten. His date was restrained, and someone covered her mouth. Brian told his girlfriend to run, and a fight ensued to free his friend. Ponz's date broke free and ran out of the tent behind Brian's girlfriend. Ponz was stabbed in the arm. As they ran to the car, the mob closely followed yelling racial epithets. Once in the car, they were quickly surrounded. He tried to drive through the crowd slowly, but the unruly crowd rocked the car; and Brian, in fear of not only his life, but the other occupants, had no choice but to hit the gas.

He lost control of the car and crashed into a curb at which time they got out and ran for their lives. The car was turned over by the mob and crushed. Some months later, all charges were dismissed, and the injured parties could not even sue him because they provoked the crime in question. Vilified in the paper, he was deemed a racist who woke up one day and decided to run over a crowd of good white folk. A retraction was never printed. Our family went through hell outside of our community. In the community, the truth was known before the verdict was contemplated. Because they knew Brian! Sometimes who you are is enough. He was a hero in New Cassel for putting his life on the line coming to the aid of his friend and their dates.

That was Mother, a die-hard friend to the end and would give her last, unless it is a food stamp. I told you she has a unnatural obsession with food stamps. Brian is not like me in that regard. One inclination of a friendship going left and I am out. If he senses something in a person, he does the complete opposite. Just remember though, loyalty to a fault can come back and bite you.

Brian is a simple man for the most part, and he appreciates simple things. A good meal, hell it can be a pot of any type of beans as long as they were prepared with smoked neck bones. Top it off with a cold can of Budweiser and a television with a remote. Baby, he'll be happier than a pig in slop. Think of a shorter black Al Bundy, and you have him. Like Mother, he is very smart and creative and pretty much a jack-of-all-trades. And will help anyone in need. He has an uncanny ability to look at something and be able to just do it.

Brian and I share a lot of the same qualities. Save for one! I am non-confrontational, but if it comes my way... He is non-confrontational and will avoid it at all cost. Especially, after what happened to Kent because he never forgave himself. Kent was a handsome young man with an aspiring basketball career. What attracted you to him, however, was his personality. He was sweet, humble, and extremely memorable because he was the complete opposite of what you expected, and shy. The kind of guy you bring home to meet your father. A son that made his single mother smile every morning she got up to fix his breakfast and step out the door to work one of several jobs to support him. Although he was the nephew of one of the mothers of Roddy's children, he remained great friends with both brothers.

He graduated from high school with a full scholarship to a Division I college. Brian and a group of their friends took Kent out to celebrate his achievements, when once again a fight broke out. Kent gave his life saving Brian from being viciously assaulted. An uninvited guest had a knife and stabbed Kent as he tried to break up the fight. He did not survive his injuries and left this world way too soon. His death did something to Brian. He blamed himself for a long time and still does on some level. His drinking binges took him to the brink of destruction. I had seen it only once before and prayed never to see it again. Brian does not handle death well. Telling him there is nothing no one can do is to no avail. He drinks himself into oblivion when someone dies. I begged him not to get drunk after we identified Uncle Charlie. The entire ride there he kept saying he knew it was not him;

he has been confused with someone else. Surfeit to say, he blamed himself for not taking Uncle Charlie home for Easter dinner. Unlike me, always wanting to fix things, he is an avoider and does not deal well with conflict. Sober that is.

I make sure I keep up with him. Even though he is a forty-seven years old and finally married that lunatic after thirty years of torture. I call her these things because for one she is crazy. And two she loves him with all his faults. There are many, for one he is cheap as hell. So I nearly fell off my seat when one day he showed up at my house with like five thousand dollars in cash.

"Why in the hell do you have so much cash on you?"

"Because she is going through my things again, and I am scared she'll find it."

"And what if she does?"

"You remember I told you I was expecting a payment from a job I did. Well, last month, it was mailed to me. She got it and bought a new car."

"So you mean to tell me you are going to walk around with thousands of dollars in your pocket."

"That's why I am here. I want you to keep my money for me."

It was not a surprise request. I am many things, but I told you before a thief is not one of them. Beside he knows I got his back. He consults me about dang near everything. I am the one who told him to take his trifling ass home and get his family mess together. Truth be told, I was also the one he asked should he marry her crazy butt. As much as I wanted to tell him to run for the hills, I wanted him to have the American dream just like everybody else. However, two days after they were married, she told him she wanted a divorce. She went down to the courthouse for some information. After talking to the clerk, the clerk told her she needed a therapist. It is my true belief that the only reason she wanted to get married is so she could tell him she wanted a divorce. I could not make this stuff up if I wanted to. They are still together, and I still have to listen to their drama every time I talk with him. Little does he know, I put the phone on mute and lay it down. I will check it from time to time, and he'll still be talking. It's wrong, but there is only so much I can take.

To know him is to love him though. Even my in-laws love him. He will stop by and tell my mother-in-law his nonsense. Recently he claimed he was passing by and decided to stop. While here, my mother-in-law asked him how his recovery was going after his hernia surgery. When he took a seat, I said a little prayer in my head for him to tell us the short version. No such luck. He told us that he had this terrible pain in his groin and private parts. The pain became increasingly worse, and he decided to go to the hospital. As he inched toward the door, his wife grabbed her pocketbook and nearly knocked him down getting out the door.

He asked, "Where are you going?"

"To the hospital with you, just in case you have some disease you'll already be there to get help after I kill you."

At the hospital, she came in the room as he was examined by two male doctors. He glanced at the female nurse who was staring at his genitals. He said he looked back at his wife in fear of her reaction. But she sat quietly. After the nurse left, a different nurse entered who told him she was there to look at the area in question. Not having had intercourse with his wife because of the hernia, as the nurse examined him he became erect. He looked back at his wife again, but she continued to sit quietly, but fidgeted. The male doctors came back in the room and told him he needed surgery. But he could do it on an outpatient basis and would be released shortly. As they waited, he told his wife that he thought the first nurse went back to the nurse's station and discussed his attributes. Shortly thereafter, a female doctor came in and told him she needed to examine him. He told her he had been released and was waiting for the nurse to remove his IV. In return the doctor said he was her patient, and she had to give him a quick exam before he was released. Brian looked at his wife, whom now, he said, looked pensive. He continued by saying that, although the doctor washed her hands she did not put on gloves. She looked at his man parts for a moment. As she reached for his who-ha, his wife, true to form, was herself. They were put out of the hospital. He said he had never been so embarrassed in his life. Even more so than the time Mother caught him smoking weed with his friends on Prospect Avenue and chased him.

My mother-in-law poured him a double shot of brandy. "You need this." She laughed until she was doubled over in pain.

Maybe the reason he stays with her is to prove that he is the opposite of the men who left Mother when her imperfections reared their ugly head. He was very much that way when we were growing up, the pacifier always wanting to make things right. But dang, I am going to keep praying for him.

I am still laughing!

Dear Roderick,

Okay, I was wrong. It is more difficult writing about you than it was Paige! I have to keep stepping away and taking a deep breath. Then I drag my feet to start again. I dreaded getting to you. But here we are. When I think of you, I think of what was, not what is. Not what the world sees, only what I want to remember. The other day I stood in my favorite sub shop, waiting for my five-dollar foot long, and I happen to glance at the television. The forthcoming story on Channel 12 News was, "Notorious Drug Dealer Holds the Hamptons Captive." I I said a quick little prayer in my head. Nope, I was not that lucky. I turned away from the television not wanting to see what is, because all I know is what was. Yes, I could have left, but I was hungry as hell. So I told myself just don't look. Not being the type of person to turn my head from anything, because as with all things, I have to see it coming. For a moment, I did not recognize you. You look so deranged and unkempt. I drift off thinking, "Dang, what happened to the half a million dollars they estimated you made?" In drug movies such as New Jack City *and* Scarface, *both the main characters were sharp as a tack. I am snapped back to reality when the owner of the sub shop starts talking to the guy behind me. Did he notice the tears rolling down my cheek and realized I love you? What he said caught me off guard, even though I only know him from frequenting his establishment; I never took him as that type of guy. Especially being foreign post 911, he should have known better not to make snap judgments about people.*

It was something to the effect of, and please forgive my paraphrasing, emotions seriously clouded my perception.

"Only in America would they let a guy like that have so many chances."

Before I realized it, I asked, "A guy like what?"

"No, I mean, you know how many times will he get arrested before he learns his lesson. This is what, his third time, they said." His accent extremely heavy, I leaned in to understand him better. "It's like lazy roaches; those people don't not want to work. In my country, man like that would be shot second time."

"First off, its do not—"

"Do not?"

"You said don't not. It is—do not. And second, how do you know he is lazy? You do not know anything about that man! Yes, what he is doing is wrong, but how can he be lazy if he is the head of the empire they say he is? I am sure it took some work on his part to maintain that position. Heavy is the head that wears the crown! You get that lazy stereotype from how black people are portrayed in the media. Finally this is not your country, so he will not be shot as you put it. He will get a fair trial in front of his peers and serve his time."

"I didn't—"

"Yes, you did! You are in here tap dancing and trying to impress these good white folk so they will keep patronizing your establishment, instead of busting out your windows again like they did after 911. To them, all you will ever be is a sand nigger who builds bombs in the back of this sub shop. They will never let you in their club. So stop it!"

"Take your sandwich and get out of my store. No, no, you keep money, and just go."

I caught the sub as it slid down the counter. Walking out of the store, the only thing I could think was, "Roddy, you motherfucker." I turned and watched as the sandwich smashed against his turban. Turkey, lettuce, tomatoes, bread just everything was on the wall and floor. People scattered out of the store, and I was with them. My last coup de grace *before I went out the door was, "Learn to speak English properly before you judge someone." I was wrong, and I knew it. Later that night, James came home and told me I was banned from my favorite sub shop. He had to give the owner one hundred dollars for the worker cleaning up the mess I made and not calling the police on me. I say all that to say I could have went to jail for defending you, again, even when you are dead wrong. To top it all off, you don't even speak to me, and I don't know the reason why.*

At heart, I will always believe that there is a basic decency and goodness, within you, though you sometimes you forget. I know if you choose to listen to it, and act on it, a great deal of what the world needs can be satisfied. It is not complicated, but it takes courage. Empathy is the courage for a person who not only listens to his own goodness, but also acts on it for someone else. Courage now is something different, and I'm not sure if you have it. But you used too. Somewhere you forgot that what is popular is not always right, and what is right is not always popular. Because of you, one of my six heroes, I'm here. But what do I know anyway? Only you know if you actually possess it. I pray you do!

You tried to fix everything. You thought it was your job to do so. I too thought it was mine also, but it wasn't. You have to look back and tell that little boy inside you to let it go, or it will destroy you. It has up until now. You have done enough time and sacrificed way too much, as we all have. Realize that what we went through is exactly that, something that happened in the past, not who we have to be today. Though weakened, you got through it, again as we all did. You are angry with me, because you think my loyalties have gone to another.

But they haven't gone to the man you think they have. Though He walks this path with me every day, and I know that my persistence to find Him did not come without cost. However, my diligence has led me to His favor. Not with worldly baubles, though there is definitely nothing wrong with that, when earned in earnest and used to bless others. But by keeping my mind, body, and soul stable during crisis, chaos, and conflict, I think Him. Think about what I have said. Write back soon, I miss you.

Love,

M—

The Unusual Suspect!

Drug movies are such a cliché. Every one of them has an underdog who aspires to get out of the ghetto. Around him, he watches the other players in the game (oh yes, it's all a game) jockeying for better positions, flash large amounts of cash, wear way too much jewelry; he surrounds himself with trashy women; he may or may not have a family at home, and of course the number one must have: fancy cars tricked out with all the ghetto accouchements he can find! All the while defending his turf, as the local police, DEA, and ATF is watching. Hell, the FDA might be there too. Don't act like you never got a free turkey off the back of a U-Haul truck from the local drug dealer during the holidays. After you got off that line, you went and got free government cheese. If you didn't, you knew somebody who did! Mother had a whole freezer dedicated to that nasty cheese. Lauren said it made the best macaroni and cheese, however. I wouldn't know I make macaroni and cheese from the box like the white folks do.

None the less, his dumb ass made exactly the same mistakes his predecessors did. Wanting his name to ring out, so he stands tall, his predilection for violence cannot be sated, or going to jail, getting high on his own supply, but more likely than not dead. Wanting to be the man has taken down the best of them. At the game that is. Now don't get this twisted; I am, by no means, condoning selling or using drugs, illegal or otherwise. Hey, in my opinion, prescription drug use far outweighs street drugs today. The only reason the spotlight is on the latter is because of who uses prescription drugs? Soccer moms do, that's who! Yeah, Pablo and "them" play soccer too, but they do not have health care. I'm just saying. You know it's true. Oh, I can tell all my business, but as soon as I say something about somebody else, I am wrong.

Once in a while, however, there comes a horseman. Somebody so unexpected, he will fly under the radar because he just does not fit the mold. Roddy was this person, in the beginning, that is. He was so much the opposite of a cliché that no matter how you tried to stuff him in that box, he wouldn't fit. If the people surrounding him had not been arrested and signed statements against him, the police would never have known what he was up to. (The first time he was arrested.) In this regard, he obviously did not pay much attention to lesson 207 at the School of Hattie Mae, because if he did, he would have never let his left know what his right was doing.

I am not sure who it was that introduced him to the drug game; some say it was one of his many girlfriends. Does it really matter at this point? He's a grown man and a predicate felon, one of many who became a product of his environment—it was the eighties, a period which has reared its ugly head too many times, in his life, and countless others'. We are losing too many of our little big brothers and big little sisters to a game that is rigged. Not to say that everyone who is from the ghetto becomes a drug dealer, because we all know that is not the case.

They grow up to become rappers/entertainers or superstar athletes. I am just playing. It is ironic however that they say the majority of drug dealers are from the ghetto. Low level, of course, with the exception of a minute few, who became successful at other endeavors. What I mean by low level is that they do not have the capabilities of flying or boating in drugs. They do not process the product from its raw state. By the time they get their hands on it, it has been processed in one form or another. So why is it that these low-level dealers are the ones who get the maximum penalties?

Know your history, people. Under the Rockefeller drug laws, the penalty for selling four ounces of heroin or cocaine, you can be sentenced from fifteen to twenty-five years to life in prison. In case you didn't know, these drug laws are named after Nelson Rockefeller, who was the New York State's governor at the time the laws were adopted. It was signed on May 8, 1973. I guarantee you that most drug dealers don't even know who he is. Throughout the years, the law continued to draw opposition because many recognized it as racist, as they apply inordinately to minorities but especially African-Americans, and to a lesser extent, Latinos. In April 2009, Governor Patterson revised these laws to remove the mandatory minimum sentences. This change allows judges to sentence individuals convicted of drug offenses to treatment or to short sentences. It makes total sense to me—drug treatment centers should include dealers. (Maybe dealers and addicts should be housed in separate wings. Or in the very least check the dealer's bag extra thoroughly.) Sentencing was made retroactive, which allows more than one thousand imprisoned convicts to apply to court to resentence and possibly release them. This mini lesson in the law is because I would be a hypocrite to pretend that I was not aware of what Roddy was doing. I feel you and I are past that. Besides, anyone who knows me knows that I enjoyed too many of the perks.

It's funny because I actually remember the day he told me. We were talking about someone we knew who was selling drugs. At first

I thought he was joking when he admitted to me that he was selling drugs. But then it made sense, all those trips to the Hamptons, wanting to drop me off at our father's house and leaving, and not quit being gone. Not for nothing, our father's house in the Hamptons was a two-hour ride from Westbury, and every time I looked up, there he was. He was in town, on certain blocks, everywhere and nowhere at the same time, but never with me at our father's house.

"Roddy, why would you want to do such a thing? If Mother finds out, and she will, she is going to kill you."

"She already knows, and I don't care."

"What? She knows, yeah right."

"Maggie, I'm grown. What can she do? Beat me."

I stood there dumbfounded. "Well, yeah."

"How do you think Fish got buried?"

"I don't know."

"You do now. I'm tired of begging people for stuff. I did what I had to (Isn't that what they all say), to make sure that *my* brother left here like a person should. I don't care what happens from here on in. If I didn't come up with the money, who would have? Nobody was going to help us."

"You don't know that?"

"Did they help with his medicine? No, that was me buying it—me! I did! Don't start crying. I have to take care of us."

"But Dad—"

"But Dad nothing! Sit down, Dad is good to *you*. He is, if you need something, he gives it to you. And that's okay with me. I don't need anything from him."

"I don't want you to go to jail or get killed."

"I'll be careful."

I walked away and cried in the privacy of my secret place. His words stabbed me in the heart like a hot dagger. Our whole world changed and not for the better. Gone were the days of our wide-eyed innocence. Sitting backward on his banana-seat bike, riding through the bicycle path, swimming at Cantiague Park in Hicksville, walking hand in hand to the "Blue store" on Prospect Avenue where the owner marveled at how Roddy followed Mother's instructions to the letter while he tended to me. She watched us cross the high-traffic four-lane streets, him struggling to hold the bag of groceries in one arm and holding on to me with the other. Like clockwork, she yelled the same thing every time, "You kids too damn small to be crossing that street by yourselves. Tell your mama I am going to report her ass one of these days." I guess she was waiting to report her after we got hit because no one ever came.

Though Roddy made sure I was not involved in his day-to-day hustle, I was slowly but surely pulled into his world of iniquity. It was marred with drug addicts, drug money, and his insatiable need to prove the world wrong. That he did matter, we all did, especially Mother. He wanted to give her all the things that he thought she deserved. But he was wrong. I am not sure what it was he thought she needed, but it wasn't baubles. Whatever it was, he couldn't provide it; none of us could. Yet there he was, in an underworld where he not only mattered—he reigned. It filled a void in him and drove his plight to right all the wrongs we endured. But somewhere along the line, that plight became a distorted and twisted game of cat and mouse. Except this wasn't a cartoon, his runs to some of the most notorious parts of uptown Manhattan like Washington Heights kept me awake at night. Have you ever watched a music video that was filmed in a grungy part of the city? (It is the same scenario for all the rappers who want to make the viewer think he was Pablo Escobar or Nino Brown in his past life.) A few guys stand at the beginning and end of the block, as well as on top of the building and appeared to be watching everything coming and going. Well, they were! Those guys were not up there playing spades, or shall I say bridge. They are the lookout and will signal to the ground patrol. God help you if you are lost and made a left when you should have made a right. You might not drive out the other end. On one city block, there may have been at least thirty apartments doing the same thing. Arros con pollo usually permeated the air as Latin beats shook the building. They might have cooked a different meal and played a different song, but the game is the game. The piss-smelling stairwell is a stereotype. Don't ask me how I know, just trust I know what I am talking about.

Up until that point, my brother had never lied to me; he told me *everything*. From what he ate for lunch, to who he boned the night before, which was usually one of my friends or someone I was acquainted with. "You don't ever want to be *that* kind of girl, Maggie!" My thing is, wasn't that girl once like me, and guys like him turned her into a girl like that? Everybody has a purpose, he would say. He didn't get it? Well, not the irony of it anyway. That was his way of keeping me on the straight and narrow. Not exactly from the Emily Post's book, *Etiquette,* I know, but it worked. Not for nothing, he too attended "the School of Hattie Mae." He never lied to me because I wasn't judgmental even though my big ole eyes might have said different. That is before she sank her fangs into him!

That white bitch destroyed so many lives. Especially after some scientist, in a high-level security government lab of course, figured out a way to transform powder into a solid. Not an addict per se, but addicted just the same—changed him so profoundly, that I no longer recognized him. I said it before, addiction make an addict of us all. Rick James said it best however: "Cocaine is a hell of a drug!" But I want to back this story up just a bit.

Dear Roderick,

My last letter came back as return to sender. Maybe the officers moved you to another facility, and the letter was mixed up in the shuffle. How are you? Mother said you have been having some health issues since you have been incarcerated. I pray this letter finds you in the best of health! So you made it to where you will be for the duration of your sentence. The last I heard you were being held over in Riker's Island Correctional Facility. *I was told that you were not happy at either place. That, this place, is much different from where you were the last time, more violent and deviant. State prisons are like that, so I've seen on television. (Laughing out loud) I'm not worried about you though, because I know you. You can get yourself out of just about anything. You probably already made friends with the biggest inmates in there. I bet you look like such the oddity when you stand with them, being that you only weigh what one hundred and two pounds wet. Just trying to make you laugh, like when we were little. Keep your head up, brother; this too shall come to pass, on the morrow!*

Use this time wisely because time does not wait for no one. Don't let your mind become imprisoned as well. Get in the library and read. Reading can take you out of your own mind, to places you have never been and may never get the chance to go. Take up a trade or a few classes. Education is always the key to freedom. It will also help pass the time, but in a positive way. It just keeps going, and before you know it, it will have passed you by.

Pray to God every day to cast out those demons that entice you to keep repeating past mistakes. Though some may think you are, you are not an animal. Only you can stop yourself from being caged like one. Not just jail, but imprisonment of the mind as well. You are a smart man, but you use your intelligence in the wrong way. Now is the time to think about all the changes you want to make to better your life when you are released. Liberate yourself of dead weight; it will continuously drag you down. I know you have a hard time realizing that everyone is not your friend. You have a good heart and that Robin Hood mentality. It has however brought down the best of them. This is a lesson I learned all too well, a long time ago. A lesson I pray you too learn before it is too late.

Stop worrying about things you cannot control. That's not a good thing to do where you are. It may cause others to see you as weak. Whatever is going to happen will happen no matter what. That is the way of life, so don't dwell on the negative things that have happened. Release them. Instead train your mind to expect good things you want to happen, and not be surprised when they do. The tongue is very powerful. Did you know you can speak into existence your desires? If you only speak negativity, only negativity will manifest.

Elevate your mind, and those around you too shall be elevated. You must understand that we are only in control of our own selves. You have to stop trying to control others as we were once controlled through manipulation. If you can't control yourself, how can you possibly ask anyone else too? I truly believe one must lead by example. If you put yourself in that position, you must hold yourself to a higher standard. Am I saying that I have all the answers? No, I am not. But I do know what doesn't work.

I have heard the rumors of your discontent with me. That I am not loyal to you this time around, and that I haven't been there for you. I may not have been there in the way you wanted me to be, and for that I apologize. It wasn't intentional. Although I must say that I am tired of this merry-go-round. I don't want to ride anymore. I'm too dizzy. However, I am always here for you, that you shouldn't doubt. You are still my brother. That is a bond I do not take lightly. I will never forget that you were there for me as I was there for you. But we are grown now, and my priorities have changed. As should yours.

Love,

M—

Back in the Days . . .

Roddy was one of the best brothers a girl could wish for. We were very close. Though four years his junior, everyone thought I was older, because I always told him what to do. And he let me. I was his little big sister; he was my big little brother. As a child, he was an unusually quiet person. It was just his personality. Most people believed he was slow, but I didn't. His thick black horn-rimmed welfare glasses against his pale skin didn't help. Not to mention he had dirty blondish hair that he never combed. It drove Mother crazy that he refused to wear the new clothes she bought him; he just preferred his old ones. No matter how tattered they were. He had no fashion sense whatsoever and did not care about getting any. When he did wear them at her behest, they didn't match. He would have on four colors with three different patterns. One could easily make the mistake that he was homeless, but the funny thing is, he took several baths a day. It was a thing with him, from what I understand he never grew out of. Freud would have loved to get him on the couch to analyze him. Roddy's mother complex would have kept Freud busy for years. Always coming to her aid, his relationship with her was a mama's boy. His poor wife!

If you watched him, he appeared to be thinking about something. Probably how to get the hell off Holly Lane. Oh, I'm sorry, that was me. Sometimes he was so deep in his thoughts he had to be called more than once. I would sit quietly by his side, trying to figure out what he was thinking. So I could think about the same thing, because it had to be something great. I told everyone that passed by, "Shhh, don't bother him. He's thinking right now." Just like that, he would snap out of it and say, "Let's go for a ride, Maggie." We would be gone for hours. Mother never had to worry about us. Even though Roddy was only ten. I didn't know that each time we crossed the Westbury railroad tracks, our lives were in danger. Third rail, what was that? I followed his lead. There was a break in a patch of bushes where he liked to cross between New York and Railroad Avenue.

He would say, "Wait here until I carry the bike across the track. I will come back to get you." Ha-Cha Stationary Store on Old Country Road, here we come. Roddy played a few games of pinball while I ate an ice cream cone, candy, or chips. Most times all three. Something Mother never allowed us to do.

We always made it home by dinner. The alternative was being locked out. Every night he sat by me at the table. He never finished all the food Mother put on his plate, which was a mortal sin. When she wasn't looking, I finished his food for him, or he would get his ass whipped. The funny thing is he would get his ass whipped for that, but not for stealing her mint 1965 cherry red Mustang, taking me along for the ride. In his younger years, he was a homebody for the most part. Nights when Mother and Tack retired early and our sibling jumped out the window to hang out, he would always create something for us to do.

He'd tap on my door and whisper, "Maggie, come on." I didn't need to know where; it didn't matter. Though not much taller than I was, he was a giant in my eyes. These were our favorite pastimes.

Stealing Mother's Mustang was the ultimate defiance. That bitch was pretty too, do you hear me? He'd let me sit in the front seat. Mind you, this was pre-seat belts. My feet didn't touch the floor, and I couldn't see over the dashboard, but I was riding. In hindsight, that car was a forbearing of what his life was to become. Fast cars, fast women, and even faster money! He drove as if he were a professional. Mother didn't catch on until the police came knocking at the door. The car had been involved in an accident, and the driver fled the scene. He looked at me. Although I didn't remember him hitting anything, I knew to keep quiet. Mother ran outside to look at her baby, and sure enough it had a huge dent in the driver side rear quarter panel. She looked at Roddy, and he took off, leaving me standing there holding the bag. Having learned my lesson about not staying put when someone else runs, I took off right behind him.

When she came upstairs to find him, she said, "Don't make me come under there to get you." He slid from under the bed. I closed my eyes anticipating what was to be the worst beat down in history. "Were you messing with my car?"

His voice quivered. "Yes, Mother." I watched her as she stood staring at him for a moment. Before she left the room, she turned and said, "Maggie, get your little ass from under that bed. I know you were riding right along with him." I wasn't crazy. I stayed put. In my mind, she was waiting for me to come out to strike two birds with one stone, or in our case one belt.

I asked from under the bed, "Why aren't we getting a whipping then?" Roddy shot me a look.

"You know I can't stand a liar! I wanted to see if he would tell me the truth."

"How did you know?"

"He ran. But he didn't wreck the car. Billy hit something in the city after he left a club. By the way, I won't be leaving the keys under the mat anymore."

"Why did Billy have our car in the city?"

"None of your business."

I believe she knew all along Roddy had been taking her car. Her little prince however could do no wrong. She did know the neighbor took the car to the city. He was gay in a town that wasn't. The only place he could freely be himself was not there. Mother was his confidant. She was one of a select few who knew his secret and was devastated by his death. He died of AIDS in the early onset of the epidemic. Although Roddy didn't judge people, he was not good at maintaining friendships like mother. Maintaining friendships and or relationships for that matter is difficult for him. These qualities emerged too late in life for him. He is a runner or avoider. As soon as the fight or flight response clicks on in the brain to protect us from the proverbial stressor, he's out. The running man wasn't just a dance craze in the eighties. The majority of his relationships, friends, or one-night stands ended that way. People who were really nice and I liked were just left by the curb. These occurrences were quit disheartening. His lack of empathy and ability to cut people off was unnerving. Many times I was the clean-up guy, by being the shoulder to cry on. Never in my worst nightmare did I think I would become one of them.

He was as straight as an arrow when he was young, a hard worker and very dependable. Except school, that was a different story. He was pretty much an outcast, struggling in many classes, with the exception of math and science. I have to give it to him. The boy has a thing for numbers, especially when they were on a piece of green paper, with a president's fact on it. He found a job at a concrete factory at twelve.

That place breathed life back into him. Across the track were primarily Italian-owned businesses. Roddy began working at the concrete company with Tack on Saturdays. He loved Tack so much and thought of him as a father. There was a period when he called him *Daddy Tack*. Tack knew how much he cared for him, but could not allow himself to be loved. Tack loved him too even if he couldn't say it. When he was angry with Mother, he used Roddy's love as a pawn and would not allow him to use the enduring term. It hurt him, but he kept trying to the very end. And I believe he is still troubled by it today. Not many people know it, but he is very sensitive. He has a strange way of dealing with emotions.

The boss of the concrete company took Roddy under his wing and gave him a permanent position. He cleaned up the primacies and ran errands. Finally he had the relationship he never had with our biological father or Tack. Many people joked about them. They called Roddy his token son. Though an odd pair for sure, Roddy never took offense to his new nickname, but the boss did. He would become irate at the thought of someone taunting him. There was an incident in which he took him to his home. As he stood outside, some boys walked past and approached Roddy. They asked him, "Aren't you on the wrong side of town, nigger?" He didn't budge. He stared quietly at them with his hands in his pocket, just waiting. In the interim, "the Boss" ran out of his house and chased them down. His family said they never saw him become physical over anything. Whatever the relationship was, it was on their terms no matter what people called them. When you saw them together, they were always laughing and happy. They gave something to each other. Maybe "the Boss" was searching also. Roddy was more focused in school and life in general. I was happy for him because he had the father he also wanted.

Unfortunately, "the Boss" had a kidney disease and died a slow painful death as Roddy watched. That was the first time he didn't run. It had the opposite effect. The sicker he became, the more Roddy retreated back into his own head, thinking. Although his demise was no surprise, the aftermath most certainly was. A piece of my brother died too—that is the brother I knew and loved. That man's death set in motion a dichotomy in his personality no one saw coming, and hell broke loose.

Dear Roddy,

How are you? I pray that you are well! Not much is going on with me. Overall I am as well as can be expected. Paige said she spoke with you last week. I asked her to tell you I have written you two letters that were returned. Are you sending them back, or are the officers not giving them to you? Since the letters are unopened, I'd like to believe they are being kept from you. I have been racking my head over how we got here? If you tell me what I did to make you so angry, I can try to make amends. We might even be able to move past it. When we were children and upset with one another, it did not last long at all.

Do you remember when we were young? We had so much fun together. I wish we could go back to those simpler times. In the very least, we would be talking. I know you probably forgot the time Mother surprised us with a trip to Rye Play Land. It was through a church group she heard about. She packed a huge lunch, and we rode the Greyhound bus. It seemed like we would never get there. But when we did, we had a ball. It was magical. We did not know where to begin. One side of the park was rides and games, and the other side was a white sandy beach. You could not get enough of the water rides. We rode so many rides I got sick. Then we played games. You won me a big red blow-up apple, and they wrote my name on it, and you won yourself a blow-up green frog. You told the man to write your name on it, but he wrote Petrified Freddy instead. I thought it was so funny, but you didn't. For me, the best part of the trip was when we picnicked on the beach. You said it was the ride home because if you had any more fun, you would float away. You laid your head in Mother's lap and fell asleep. I watched you as you slept. Mother smiled as she stroked your hair, as she gazed out the window. She asked, "Did you have a good time, Maggie?"

I answered, "The best," and I asked if we could go again.

She continued smiling. Her skin glowed in the warm light of the setting sun. "It's so beautiful up here. Look at how big the houses are. It would take two of me a whole day to clean one of them."

"Mother, one day I will buy you a big house just like that one, and someone will clean it for you."

"If you say you are going to do it, then I know you will do it."

The ride home was so peaceful. I remember thinking what life would be like if we lived there. Would I have been a cheerleader, or an equestrian? Would you have played lacrosse or field hockey? Would we have hung out at the local mall or have been carpooled to school, instead of taking the stretched yellow limousine to and from school every day. It sat forty-two people; and we had, well not door-to-door service, but we were picked up and dropped off on the corner of our block. The streets there were empty. No children playing double Dutch or four corners outside, no drunks sleeping on the side of the store, no drug dealers standing on the corners, or cars with loud stereo systems polluting the sterile neighborhood air with idiot noise.

Just big beautiful houses crowned the tops of rolling knolls adorned with beautiful flowers and mature trees. As the ride lolled on, the quiet became deafening. After I picked out my house and car and day-dreamed three different versions of what if, I got bored as hell. By the time we reached our neighborhood,

Man Man and drunk Mike, sitting on the side of the two o'clock store, and Big Tittie Dot and Uncle Charlie staggering down Prospect Avenue were all a welcome sight.

I realized that this was our reality. I could no more understand the reality of those people living in one of those big fancy houses than someone from their community understanding ours. But it was fun dreaming. If but for a moment, I stepped outside the mundane and reinvented myself. You should try it sometimes.

Love,

M—

The Mad Scientist: In the Hood, E Does Not Equal mc Squared; It Equals Microphone Check One, Two, One, Two

If Isaac Newton's three laws of motion are correct in the premise that describes the relationship between the forces acting on a body and its motion is due to those forces, then from a philosophical standpoint, they actually make sense when it comes to Roddy.

We all know that law number one states, an object at rest will remain at rest, and an object in motion will remain in motion, in a straight line that is, unless acted upon by an unbalanced force—Physics 101, right? Basically the unbalanced force for Roddy was the death of the boss and then Richard, thus setting him on a path of destruction. Selling drugs, promiscuity, and indifference is a cocktail for disaster. In 1988, Mother was hospitalized for a bleeding ulcer, due to her drinking. The doctor informed the family that she had a 60-40 percent chance of surviving because she became septic. I was away at college, and instead of Roddy coming to pick me up, he left me stranded. I had to find a ride from Westchester County back to Long Island with no money for gas or tolls. Unaware I was coming; I arrived home to find him having a party. The house was filthy. The first thing I did was clear out everyone who was not only partying but actually living there in Mother's absence. Next I started cleaning. I decided to start with my room because it was late and I was exhausted. My plan was to attack the rest of the house the next day and then go visit Mother. To my surprise, I found my room otherwise occupied. Judging from the occupants, the sheets needed to be burned, not washed. After stripping the bed, I began vacuuming, and this small white-and-blue bottle with red writing rolled from under the dresser. Naturally I thought it was deodorant, so I walked it up to the evicted occupant. As I handed it over to him, I noticed the word *RID* was highlighted in red octagon. Above it was written for the treatment of . . . Suffice it to say, I slept on the living room floor that night.

Law number two states an unbalanced force acting on an object causes it to change its velocity in the direction of the force. Unable to properly deal with the despair of those deaths, and Mother's brush with near death, was the catalyst for the unbalanced force acting on an object, caused Roddy to become reckless and callous. Therefore, his directional force changed from Robin Hood to Nino Brown. After being released from the hospital, Mother moved back to Tack's house. But Roddy and I chose to remain at the house on Broadway. At first, I believed it would be great to live with him when I would come home for vacations. That is until he started bringing his work home with him. One night, he called me at two or three in the morning and said, "I am on my way home. Rock Rock and Chef are with me. Get up and cook us something to eat." Not for nothing, Blaze, Chef, Rock Rock, and them were cool people and all, but outside the house.

Don't judge me until someone walks off with your favorite pocketbook with damn near everything you own in it, even your birth control pills. What was I supposed to do for the next month or so? You cannot miss one of those little bastards, more or less, three weeks of them! I have not had a natural method of anything since like the sixth grade. I have a relaxer in my hair and welcome preservatives in my food. I am not a good dancer, so I am not down with the Rhythm Method. Take my temperature every day, for what? I don't have a fever. *Pull out?* Are you crazy? You know the cream filling is the best part of a Twinkie! It was one of those sticky-fingered motherfuckers Roddy brought home with him, who just couldn't help himself. Have you ever heard the saying you can't make a hoe into a housewife? Well, you can't make a crack head into a houseguest. It's the same premise, but different context.

I moved back with Mother and Tack the next day. Roddy began spending money like water. A lover of the brand, he purchased a new 1988 Ford Mustang GTO 5.0 out of the showroom. Cherry red, of course. Showing off, he picked me up from one of my many temporary jobs. After getting in, I realized my new coat was caught in the door. Just as I opened it, a car came out of nowhere and took the whole door off. If he did not pull me in, I would have been taken right along with it. To say he was angry was an understatement. He had that car three hours if that, and it was damaged, which lead to the following.

Law number three states for every action, there is an equal and opposite reaction. Some people believe that the legalization of drugs will eradicate crimes associated with drugs. That since there is a mutual reciprocation, then selling drugs is a victimless crime and a waste of police services. Well, until that day comes employers of said occupation better keep a lawyer on retainer. The first time he was arrested was less than two weeks after Richard died. By the time he was arrested, his behavior had become so erratic I was grateful. Richard's death did something to him. I will neve forget that day.

"The police are coming to arrest me, and I need you to be here when they get here."

"No, I'm not coming. It's too damn early."

"And don't tell Mother."

I threw on some clothes and ran out of the house with no coat. March in New York can be like sitting on a block of ice bare butt. By the time I pulled up, police cars were already there. I got out, and an officer stopped me from entering the yard.

"I'm Roderick's sister. Can I please see him before you take him away? I need to ask him if I should have our mother contact his attorney."

Confused, the officer looked at me like I had two heads and turned his back to me and said something into his radio. I am standing there freezing.

Soon after, Roddy and his girlfriend, Valerie, came walking out of the house. Though happy, I was bewildered as to why he didn't have handcuffs on and was not accompanied by an officer.

I grabbed him and held him tightly. "What's going on?"

"I have to tell you some bad news."

"What?"

He stared at me for what seemed like an eternity. His mouth kept trying to formulate the words. It was when his eyes welled with tears that I screeched, "What is it, dammit?"

"Richard died in his sleep last night."

"Yeah right? Stop playing and tell me." We stood in an awkward silence looking at one another waiting for the other one to break their gaze first. I took off running for the door and made it past the officer, but was stopped short at the sight of my brother. I can't tell you much else that happened after that because I don't remember. I have always had this gift of shutting down in stressing situations. The only thing I do remember is telling Roddy to go get Mother.

I kept telling everyone something was not right with him. He seemed off, but I could not put my thumb on exactly what it was. Mother said to leave him alone because he was just sad. We were all sad, but this was different. Believing Richard's death was his fault, he traveled down a path of destruction. After his arrest, he stopped eating. While on bail, I watched him closely. I sat next to him during the service. It wasn't surprising that what seemed the entire town came to pay their respects. I don't think Roddy noticed. He was somewhere else, somewhere distant I couldn't reach him. After the service was over, we were in a car accident.

Gaunt, his weight loss made him look as if he was terminally ill. He had given up on life. I think going to jail saved his life.

After his death, Richard came to me in my dreams, but I was not ready to accept him in that form and at that time in my life. He had a message he wanted me to give Brian and Roddy. Every night, he would be standing by my closet. I would wake up screaming and in a cold sweat. To say I became sleep-deprived is an understatement. It sent me on a downward spiral fast. I did not care about anyone especially myself, so I drank myself numb. Staying out late, meeting the sun as it ascended, and I descended into the abyss of my mind. Completing college became a distant memory; therefore I got a job to support myself. Richard kept coming, and coming, and coming.

One night, a friend of the family called me and said he was in desperate need of money and was selling his family's wine and liquor collection. Brian found me passed out in my room covered in a puddle of puke. When I came to my senses, I gave him the message. Not giving the message to Roddy kept Richard coming, and I kept spiraling. My entire support system crumbled beneath me. No one was there to press the stop button. I had to save myself.

In jail, Richard started visiting Roddy, and it freaked him out. He was sent to the infirmary. Richard stopped visiting him and came back to me until I finally gave him the message against the wishes of Mother. I went to the Yapank jail by myself and sat down with him and took his hands in mine.

"I have something I need to tell you."

"Is Mother okay?"

"Yes, everybody is fine. It is about what you have been dreaming." He tried to pull away.

"I do not want to talk about that!"

"Lower your voice, inmate," the guard by the doorway shouted.

"Listen to me, sit down."

The guard walked over to us. "Do we have a problem here?"

"No, sir."

"If we do, your visit will be terminated immediately."

"No, sir. Everything is fine, sir."

"Well then, keep it down."

In my head I said, "Damn, we heard you the first time." He sat back down.

"Mag, I do not want to talk about this."

"Let me talk then. Don't be afraid. Richard gave me a message to give to you. He came to me in my dreams, and I know he also came to you. He said he will not stop until I give it to you."

After that, he never came back again. I know you're asking what the message was, but he asked me to tell Brian and Roddy, not the world. Sorry!

There was an older guy in jail that I know God sent to Roddy as a guardian angel. He took him under his wing and literally forced him to eat even if he had to feed it to him. Every night before he went to bed, he made him eat a thick peanut butter and jelly sandwich and wash it down with two glasses of milk. It may not sound like much, but it worked. In the morning, the guy forced him to get out of bed and shower; there were days he rolled him out of bed and dragged him in the shower fully clothed. Wherever he is today, I would like to thank him for forcing my brother to live.

Many things went wrong for Roddy; it would seem all at the same time. Although, I believe in the law of an equally opposite reaction happening to you, Richard's death was not on him. Everything he acquired however through ill-begotten means was fair game, and that was the reason they were taken away from him.

Death is to life as life is to death, necessary. It is a difficult part of life that is unfortunate. We tend to have trouble dealing with the passing of a life in terms of letting go and moving forward, instead of rejoicing in the fact that that person is at peace and no longer in pain. But you have to.

Dear Roderick,

Although I pray you are well, this will be my last letter. I have written you several times to no avail. Mother said she gave you the messages that I am trying to contact you. She told me to leave you alone, that you would contact me when you are ready. First of all, I did not know I was bothering you. Second, I do not want to run out of time. I really need to speak with you. What I need to tell you cannot be said in a letter, especially a letter that others read. And also, letters that come back to me in the mail.

I have been thinking about you so much lately. Your birthday is in a few days, and I guess I was reminiscing about when we were young. Mother loved celebrating our birthdays. She always made them special. Remember she would bake a cake; it was always the same, yellow with chocolate frosting. Oh and dinner, she always made a huge dinner. Fresh bread from scratch and ice tea, which was welcomed considering we usually had a choice between milk and water. You know I don't drink tea now, milk either. It's funny though I miss her baked bread. I bet I know what you miss, her honey-glazed ham, green cabbage, and rice! Is your mouth watering? That is probably the only dinner I did not have to eat for you.

The other day, I rode through New Cassel. It had been a long time since I had been there. Albeit I was driving down Prospect Avenue, I barely recognized where I was. I had to pull over and take stock of exactly where I was. The old town had gone through some major gentrification. The dilapidated low-income four-plex on the corner of Prospect Avenue and Hopper Street has been replaced with beautiful brown stones. In the place of the two o'clock store now sits a community employment agency. They made the best whiting fish sandwiches you ever tasted. What truly surprised me was the Blue Store was no longer blue! Nor was it owned by the Warfield family. Now it is a stucco bodega. As I drove past I almost expected Mrs. Warfield to step out of the store and say, "Tell ya mama I'm still going to report her ass."

I must admit I did get a bit emotional when I saw a Cassel Concrete truck. I started smiling as I thought about Tack rushing home to use the bathroom. He would exit just as quickly as Mother handed him a brown paper bag. The contents were practically scoffed down as he walked out the door. How I loved you and the Boss coming to pick me up for lunch. Do you remember that time when the two of you drove me to Dad's house and he cursed you out? I had never seen him behave like that. I believe he was jealous. Sweet memories I wish we could laugh about together. I will never give up on you or stop loving you. When you are ready, I will be here waiting. But don't take too long. Tomorrow is promised to no one.

M-

A Lesson Not Learned Is Still a Lesson, Right?

Fortunately, Roddy didn't get much jail time. Since it was his first-time offense, he was able to join the Shock Incarceration program. Ultimately this program was developed to lessen prison time by way of a military-style boot camp for nonviolent offenders. Its aim is to foster substance abuse treatment, academic education, and other help to promote their reintegration into the community. At his graduation, I watched his class march in unison, yes, sir, no, sir, and answer on command all the while thinking what a bunch of poppycock! Why couldn't you behave this way at home? You would not be here in the first place. It was all just a big show, and for what? To prove that our good tax money was being wasted on societal deviants who when given the chance would most likely repeat the same offense that landed them in jail in the first place.

When he was released, he hit the ground slinging his poison one hundred miles and running. It was as if he had never left. Roddy's descent into the drug subculture took a toll on our relationship. After his second arrest, I had to distance myself. He and anyone associated with him had become pariahs. Long gone were the perks I once enjoyed being his sister. No more walking in clubs without waiting on long lines or receiving complimentary drinks from strangers. Robin Hood had become public enemy number one. One month before his arrest, I was at Club Sapphire in Easthampton with several friends when I noticed how the tide had changed. It was a small intimate club that had become a favorite of mine and had a relaxed vibe I like. We were sitting at our favorite table, and everyone was laughing and drinking except me. Tom excused himself from the table to go smoke some weed with a girl he had just met. Not a bodyguard per se, but I usually traveled with one or two of the guys that worked for Roddy. Other friends meandered to the dance floor when the music stopped and the light turned on.

As I sat there wondering what was going on, three of the biggest bouncers I have ever seen walked over to the table. Another guy small in stature squeezed between them and asked, "Are you Roddy's sister?"

"Yes, I am." Nervous but trying to play it cool, I sipped the drink in front of me. "Why?"

"I want you out of my club right now! You and all your drug-dealing friends have two minutes to clear out of here before I call the cops."

"Are you serious?"

"Do I look like I am joking? My friends here can help you out if you need assistance."

"Do we have a problem here?" Tom asked as he approached the table just as shocked as I was.

"No, there's no problem. We have been asked to leave, and that is what we are going to do." I turned to the owner and added, "And your assistance will not be necessary. We will go peacefully."

The next day, Roddy stopped by, and I told him a storm was approaching, and he needed to get out of the game. But he did not heed my warning. He was not as lucky that time around and lost five years of his life in prison. While there, he did not sit idle. He took a couple of courses and received licenses in several trades. I visited him every other day and wrote him a letter every day, even if it was just about the weather. Yes, it was daunting, but I wanted him to know he was loved and not forgotten.

After his release, he got married and started his own printing company. Against advice from everyone in the family, he bought Tack's house and moved his family there. For a couple of years, he did quite well. Old ghost and the allure of what was was too enticing for him to resist. And therefore we end where we began!

Rebirth

Though your love molded me into this fabulous neurotic freak you are reading about, I had to walk through the fire, yet I am here! Consumed by the flame, albeit I was not burned. Not knowing why, I set fire to everything I touched and walked away as it consumed everything it embraced.

I walk quietly through life now, no longer feeling as if I have to stomp with every spiritual step I take toward His light. My rebirth has been quite the conundrum. Those to whom I once dedicated my life question if this too is just another face. If it is, I beg for it to last a lifetime. What I was doing before was not working. Now the imprecation has been lifted, and I know what it means to be free. Free to be all the things I wanted to be but was afraid. Some days I am Clair Huxtable and June Cleaver, baking cookies just because and being the classroom mother. Being that my children only played soccer for maybe two summers, I have also been a basketball mom (one summer, my son has no coordination) and the gymnastic mom (less than a summer, like me, my daughter likes to eat. Although she will be upset with me for saying this, thick girls don't make good gymnast.) With all the new clubs and sports they tried, I became someone new, but the core always remained the same. But even then, perfection was always the goal. And though I hate to admit it, my mother-in-law was right. I drove myself crazy being all things . . . It took me dying on a bathroom floor and being reborn in his light to realize what is important. (It is not as nasty as it sounds however.) After all that, I realized the detriment I was doing to myself. Now at peace, I see the beauty in the simplest things: Paige's unconditional love, Richard, the best big brother a girl could wish for, Ann's quest for me to be more, Lauren's acceptance of me, no matter what, Brian's always trying to make me happy—even if it was not always legal, and Roddy keeping me safe from harm.

I was so caught up in what not to do and what Mother went through I forgot where I was going. Off the beaten path, I became very dark. It was in the still of the night, the devil was busiest, entering my mind and causing confusion. The darker I became, the brighter I shone. The great illumination led others like me to follow. Wherever I went, there I was. Another face! Life plays out on the road you travel. So I learned to read the signs.

Remember sometimes you can take a wrong turn and find yourself going down the most god-awful stretch imaginable, spinning your wheels and praying it's not a dead end. Well, I say if it is a dead end, turn around and keep driving. God will always provide you with an off-ramp!

Hattie-isms taught to me at "*The School of Hattie Mae*"

Warning: Do not use! They didn't help me—and I am sure they will not help you either!

- First and foremost, "Self-preservation is key!"
- Under any circumstances, Maggie, never, ever, tell our personal business!
- Never let your left know what your right is doing.
- Always do your dirt by your damn self, Maggie!
- Come up with your own stupid shit to do.
- If I'm caught—we all caught.
- Never give your love away for free, because even douche cost money.
- You can't trust anyone, not even your own shadow. One day you'll be standing in the sun, and that bitch will be stabbing you in the back.
- Fuck "Plan B"; you better have a C and D ready!
- Always have a private stash that no one knows about. There will come a day when you may have to run. It's called a "Runaway Fund." Try to have at least $500 in it at all times. It won't get you as far as you would like, but it will get you far enough to be safe from what you are running from.
- Falling in love is a luxury I can't afford.
- Happily ever after only exists in movies.
- Technicalities, semantics, the little things, all the pieces matter!
- When you fuck up, fuck up big!

- When doing dirt, make sure no one is watching!
- A good lie is better than a truth no one wants to hear any day.
- Never say never!
- You can only save yourself.
- Keep your enemies close, your friends even closer, and feed all their asses with a long-handled spoon!
- Cry in the privacy of your own secret place. If they see you cry, they win.
- First impressions are everything, so give it your all.
- If they are going to talk about you, give 'em something to talk about.

Acknowledgements

First and foremost, I know nothing is possible without my Lord and Savior Jesus Christ!

Xlibris thank you so much for continuing to make my dream into a reality.

The last three years have been extremely difficult. For our daughter's sixteenth birthday my husband and I were taking the family to *Serendipity* in Manhattan, New York to celebrate. By the time we arrived I literally could not get out of the car. My body was not responding to what my brain was telling it to do. I was diagnosed with multiple autoimmune disorders. The specialist told me this occurs in less than 10% of the population. It took some time to settle in that mortality was staring me in the face. Life as I knew it would never be the same! Although it has been a constant uphill battle, I choose to fight. I would like to thank those who have encouraged me along the way—

To my husband James aka "Big Sexy" You are still BIG, and you are still SEXY! I want to say thank you for staying by my side, especially when the hour became darkest. My children: Allanah you and that iphone will rule the world. Thanks for being my biggest cheerleader and on the hunt for my cure. You have grown into a beautiful young woman who knows what she wants **- GO GET IT!** James Jr. you are growing up so fast. I love that you are not a follower, but a leader. Can we say future President? A mother can dream.

My Mother Hattie Mae the catalyst for all my shenanigans, I love you.
Yes I am my brother's keeper. Priscilla, Richard, Annette, Lisa, Bernard, and Freddie please don't kill me!
Maggie, I don't say it enough thank you, thank you, thank you for being not only the best mother-in-law, but my friend. Pops I love you, you crabby patty.
Dad you are a silver fox, Tammy and the entire Stephens family much love.
Continued Peace & Blessings to all my extended New Cassel families.

P.S.
If there is anyone I left out, you know I love you!

American Autoimmune Related Diseases Association, Inc
22100 Gratiot Avenue
East Detroit, MI 48021
586.776.3900
586.776.3903 (fax)
800.598.4668
(Literature Request)

For a look back at Maggie Stephens-Dykes previous work read:

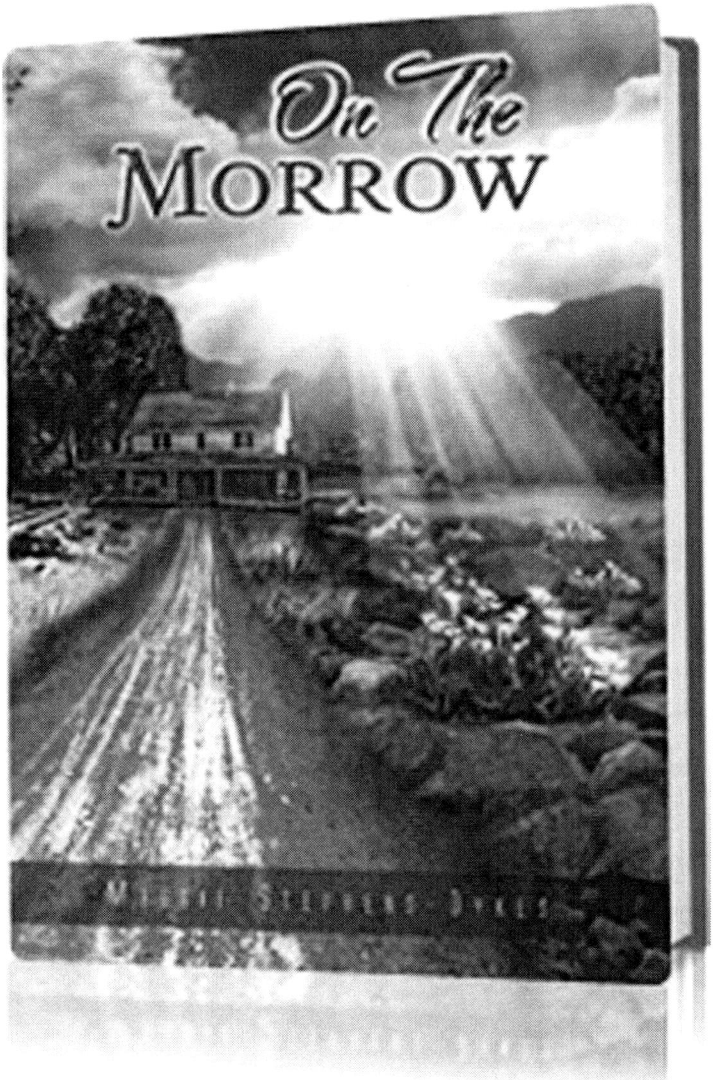

To read an excerpt of her upcoming book

"A Place of Repose"

just turn the page!

A Place of Repose

Inspired By True Events

By Maggie Stephens-Dykes

Today is July 1st; it has to be the absolute worst day of my life, for the reason that my world has changed. Although I should start at the beginning as all things must, I am not going to tell you everything now, in time I will, but not now because that would surely ruin the journey! Besides, I am not ready to say the words. I pray that by the time I am finished, you will understand why I did what I did. Something happened I did not intend, and much that once was, will soon be lost. Things that I do not want forgotten could quite well be lost, after this. You will never forgive me. Unfortunately for us there will not be a happy ending. Not for this! Yes I know it is a sin, but I pray that God, and one day you too, can forgive me.

I have decided to document it, for the children. It is important for them to know the truth, at least my version of it anyway. Hey, you once told me that there are always three versions of the truth; mines, yours, and what can actually be proven. Not to say that you will not do me justice, but I understand there will be times when my name is not be spoken. At least not in vain, as well as pictures of me taken down from walls I painted. Do you remember I drove all the way to New Jersey in that severe thunder storm to find just the right shade of khaki? Who was it that told me about that little paint store anyway? Marci did, that's right. Who knew there were so many variations on the color wheels? At first you did not like that color. I kept telling you wait until the house was completely decorated before you judged it. Look at me, just rambling on. I guess I just do not want to be erased from aspects of our life. Or shall I say the history of us. You know?

It is in these instances that history can become legends, and legends, a myth. I do not want that. The children should know me, no matter what. The sin I am committing is mine not theirs. Please do not punish them for what I have done. Let them get to know me. Otherwise, they will grow to hate you for that, and that is not my intent.

I hope you continue to use some of this stuff after I finish telling you what I need to tell you. Or at least give it to the children. It would be a shame to let it go to waste. I never knew they were so dang expensive. To top it all off, it was such a hassle to set it up. I should have let the clerk do it at the store. But noooo! You know me always something to prove. How many times have you said, "You are too strong for your own good? It's okay to let people in to help you, sometimes!"

Well I should have taken your advice today; it took way too long to get this thing working. Now I do not have as much time as I would like to say what I need to say. Unfortunately for me it means I have to rent this room one more extra day than I planned. Uh, well, I do not really mind. It is funny you know. All these years I never paid this hotel any attention. That is, before this. Despite the fact that the outside is so unassuming, it is quite nice on the inside, and tranquil. There's a huge Jacuzzi tub. I am so going to use it as much as possible. I wanted to take advantage of it before I spoke with you today to relax my nerves a bit. Regrettably I am running out of time. You of all people know how I love Jacuzzi tubs! Oh well, there is always next time. Room nine nineteen. I have to write that number down so I can request it again.

Oh be quiet don't even think about raising that red flag in your head and say, "There goes your fear of new things again."

This time I can honestly say I get a good feeling in here. Blame it on the Fung Shui. At any rate, let me get to at least part of why we are here! Oh jeeze will you look at the time, I have to get home to make dinner. Tonight is roast leg of lamb, garlic mashed potatoes, and asparagus, yum-o. Homemade iced tea, and for desert, peach cobbler with a scoop of vanilla ice cream! You know I actually feel hungry. I might even be able to keep it down. Maybe it was our talk. I thought I would feel worse once this process began, but I actually feel much better. Talk to you again soon!

CPSIA information can be obtained at www.ICGtesting.com
Printed in the USA
BVOW021056110313

315223BV00001B/26/P

9 781479 748594